Furnace

Dragon

Prologue

Summer of 1985

A Research Center in Los Angeles, California

Fernando was a Mexican Marathon runner with potential, but he had an encounter with the law, which destroyed all his prospects. It is usually people in this type of scenario that are easily swayed when offered an illicit opportunity.

Fernando saw the advert in the newspaper kind of by accident. It said that he could apply to the agent whose phone number was featured, and that he stood a chance to make a new life in America. The only snag was that this was an illegal venture and that he would only be able to go back to Mexico when he'd fulfilled his duties towards the Athletic Society who was paying for the procedures that were to be performed on his genetic structure, as well as for his training.

Fernando had to think long and hard, though, when it came to leaving his family behind in Mexico. But what swayed him was the 1 Million US Dollars that was to be his reward for participating in the program. They also agreed to pay out the amount directly to his family in Mexico, should something happen to him while he was in America.

The fact of his criminal record closed the deal. Should this deal be successful, he would be able to begin a complete new life...

We meet up with Fernando on a half marathon track that was worked out specifically for marathon runners. They wanted to test his potential after the procedure where his genome was interfered with reached completion.

After pushing himself a bit more than he was supposed to according to the program, he lost consciousness.

Fernando was as excited as any person who had just received a complete new life.

The actual preparation and in-depth training would continue on the Monday after the following Friday, when the after-procedure tests would be finalized.

*****

His coaches gave him the go-ahead to do some exercises, cautioning him not to overdo it. They said the stiffness after the previous day's exercises will gradually subside after a few days...

"Life in Abundance,' they called it." He said to nobody in particular. "So let's give it a shot and see..."

*****

"Just don't push yourself too hard," said Luis, the head coach, as he attached the equipment that was necessary to monitor Fernando's vital signs and keep track of him.

"You got it, Coach!" replied Fernando. "I will make sure everything is as it should be..."

*****

And now, here he was, on the track.

"How I've missed this," he said, once again, to nobody in particular. "But it's all proven to be worth it..."

Fernando stooped in preparation, then took off.

I'll first do two rounds as a test,' he thought. 'If it looks and feels fine after that, I'll do four...'

The track they gave him to do his rounds was marked out specifically for middle distance half-marathon runners. They said he could go back to long distance marathons as soon as he's proven to be fit for middle distance...

The sensors on his chest monitored his breathing and oxygen level, as well as his heart rate. There also was a tracking device in Maitlon it was necessary to find him, should the urgently needed to assist him for whatever reason...

The track was eight miles from beginning to end, after which he was to turn around and retrace his steps. Pretty straight forward, with no ups or downs of more than five degrees. Any fellow competitors would have to do the same distance and/or terrain during practices... that's if they were anticipated to compete on the same level...

After about one mile, Fernando found the track somewhat tedious. He wasn't even slightly out of breath. It felt as though he was taking a stroll to the grocery store on the corner...

'I know this was supposed to be a simple test,' thought Fernando, 'and that I wasn't even supposed to work up even a little bit of a sweat while running, but this is ridiculous...'

He stepped it up a little, and it felt great getting back into real action. But he was impatient. He really felt fantastic, and wanted to put his new vital body to the test...

'This being a nice Autumn day,' he thought, 'I won't be in danger of over heating and run into trouble. I wonder if I should pick it up a little..?'

Fernando felt ready for some real tough exercise.

'Why not?' he thought. 'They threatened to harm my son, but would they really go that far?'

Fernando was quite certain that they wouldn't hold true to their words of coercion. After all, they'd have to go to Mexico to reach his family. They'd specifically brought Fernando over from Mexico to do this experiment. And he knew that they'd paid his reward for allowing this over to his wife, so financially, they were fine...

'I think they've voiced those threats in Maitlon I'd try to get away from the experimental procedures,' he reasoned. 'But they have no fear of that now, do they? Picking this up a little won't do any

harm, I'm sure... I think I might even earn something extra for taking the initiative to put the 'new body' to test...'

Fernando kept running at the same speed, still wondering whether he should- or shouldn't do this.

'Oh! What the heck...' he thought *"I'm gonna do this. What do I have to lose?'*

Fernando began to virtually sprint. Everything in his body worked like a well-oiled mechanical mechanism. He stooped low against the breeze that was blowing from the front.

Then he ran faster.

'Still no significant sign of getting tired,' he thought. *'Wonder what will happen if I'd really actually sprint the rest of the way...'*

And he put action to his thoughts...

Fernando had been into athletics since his school days. This was the first time ever that he'd engaged into this type of exertion during a long distance track without getting out of breath...

'I think if this was measured,' he thought, *'it would go down in the history books as a world record. Not even the current record holders would be able to equal this... Come to think of it... wasn't the USA currently doing a study on how to help all high-level athletes to compete in globally encouraged high-stamina sporting activities?'*

Fernando arrived at a slight upward slope. Holding his breath, he'd increased his speed a little to allow for the minor bit of strain his body would experience against the breeze, which was now coming down at an angle from the right. In spite of the slope and the effect of the breeze, Fernando didn't slow down at all, which was already amazing.

Ecstatic, he took the track like he was on a level straight, still sprinting... or rather flying... like never before...

Suddenly, just before the slope would end on the turning point to return to the starting point, Fernando began to sweat profusely and he started to hyperventilate. His heart began to beat like crazy. Then he experienced a sharp pain in his head, and then another sharp pain in his chest. All went dark around him so he couldn't see a thing.

Confused, he tried to blink, but to no avail. Everything remained dark…

Then he lost his balance and hit the soil at a massive speed for a marathon runner…

Fernando landed uncomfortably and cartwheeled down a slope to he left of the track, coming to a stop against a large tree. He was slightly aware of multiple injuries all over his body, but that was the least of his concerns. He attempted to breathe, but couldn't get any air into his lungs. As he breathed out for the last time, all went black. He lost his consciousness and was totally oblivious to what was happening around him…

After a while, he briefly regained his consciousness. Unable to move, he just lay there until he heard voices. Opening his eyes, he realized that it wasn't dark around him anymore, but that his vision was blurred. He didn't know how long he'd been lying there in that condition. It must've been hours, since the shadows of the trees seemed longer.

Through his blurred vision, he saw people but didn't recognize them. About four people, by the looks of it…

They picked him up, put him on a stretcher, carried him a distance and then unceremoniously flung him into the back of a van… They spoke Spanish, so he understood what they were saying.

'They must be from my country, then,' he thought. 'So they must be taking me back to the research center… or to the hospital…'

His last awareness before falling unconscious again, was that of being in a moving vehicle.

'They must be taking me back,' was his last though before totally losing his consciousness for the last time ever…

*****

At the lab, they switched off all devices that were connected to Fernando.

"It was a success," declared a scientist. "The alarm had sounded and we knew precisely where to find him."

"Too bad we lost him, though," said another scientist, a female. "He'd shown some enormous potential..."

"Let's call it 'collateral damage,'" replied the first scientist. "You win some, you lose some..."

"Yip!" said the second scientist. "we were fortunate that nobody from the public had seen him fall. He would've been taken to a hospital where the fact of the experiment would've been discovered by some specialist..."

"Yes, that's true," replied the first scientist. "A blessing in disguise, I should say..."

*****

During autopsy, they'd discovered a whole series of anomalies, but nothing they hadn't seen before. He was running much too fast for that stage of the experiment. Too bad he was lost, but the scientists Knew they had other subjects waiting, so they weren't too concerned. They would just continue where they'd left off when the next subject takes this one's place.

"It still is a pity, though," said the female scientist. "He did show a lot of potential, since he'd been a long-standing marathon runner before the police nabbed him for drug peddling..."

What used to be Fernando was transferred to an ICU unit. Although there was no brain function and he was declared brain dead, the body had to be kept alive until the pathologist arrived.

Fernando, now brain dead, lay unconscious on an examining table. The life support equipment remained hooked onto him, since the vital organs had to be kept in a working condition, doing their work. The pathologist still needed to investigate to find out precisely what went wrong. This, in spite of the fact that at that point, they'd already had a very good idea...

This body, like a few others on the premises, were to be kept in this condition for as long as it could be utilized. The man's blood was running through a system that extracted it and repacked it into small samples, eliminating all unnatural components, then pumped it back into the body to be mechanically circulated indefinitely.

The pathologist entered the room and took some samples so that he could perform biopsies on them. Samples were taken from the brain, heart, spleen, liver, a lung and a kidney.

Upon examining the spleen sample and the lung sample under the electron microscope, the pathologist found that the capillaries were blocked by a substance that looked like a multitude of little spiders.

"This must be the reason for his collapse." He said to the lab technician standing next to him. "Please get hold of the boss wherever he is in Nevada. I need to speak to him right away."

The tech nodded, walked to the cubicle that served as an office, and picked up the red landline phone, which was a direct line to the boss...

*****

Fernando was offered the world on a platter, but six weeks later, he was dead. He was promised ultimate fame and fortune. Instead, he'd lost his life, as well as his dignity.

Rest in peace, Fernando...

Short Prelude - Despair

Midsummer 1987

Manhattan – Los Angeles - California

On a scorching, clammy mid-summer afternoon in Los Angeles, California, a girl found herself in her upper-middleclass home, in her bedroom, frustrated and close to tears. Frantically, she attempted over and over to inject her daily 'fix.'

Having been addicted for two years already, therefore displaying tough scar tissue over most of her left arm, she found it near impossible to locate a vein into which she could stick the hypodermic needle. Each unsuccessful attempt wasted another small, precious, drop of her 'dragon,' the drug 'heroine ...'

The drug was her only hope of escaping the pain that was already taking over her body.

A single dose bought, spending her lunch money on it.

While most other kids bought 'tuck' with their lunch money, she was limited to how much heroine, also called 'Smack,' she could get for her fifty bucks.

Of course, her parents were unaware of her habit, and the hell she was going through as a result of it. Had they known, she would have been lucky to have understanding parents... most addicted teenagers didn't...

Copious perspiration running down her entire body, she had the chills, nonetheless.

Her skin felt as if she had insects crawling underneath it.

She was cramping all over.

She felt fragile and nausea was threatening to take over, emptying whatever she still had in her stomach since breakfast.

She was hyperventilating and her heart felt like it was about to take off and leave her body, so fast was her heartbeat.

Her body demanded relief from the pain that was terrorizing her.

'I'd better get this done now,' she thought, panicking. 'Don't think either of my parents would help me out with cash for a 'fix.' Oh! How I wish I'd never started... but it's too late... and how I wish I could end this... but that's near impossible...

Suddenly, her thoughts cleared up... she'd found the vein at last... she felt the bitter-sweet liberation as relief gushed through her body, displacing the pain.

She heaved a sigh of relief...

Her heart rate returned to normal and her perspiration dried up.

'I desperately need a shower, right now,' she thought as she made her way to the bathroom to get herself cleaned up...

*****

A week later, the girl bought a fix from an unethical pusher and overdosed... Having been in the presence of acquaintances when it happened, she was taken to a nearby hospital and was pulled through...

Section I – Judy

Chapter 1 – A Dragon called Heroine

Judy was just your normal teenage girl, until she got hooked up with a 'dragon.' This 'dragon' was in the process of completely destroying her life.

Many young people, most of which are school age teenagers, encounter this 'dragon' some time during their lives.

Judy could've gotten through it without much of a problem, had her parents been there for her as they should've been…

*****

Midsummer, Friday, July 24th, 1987.

LA, California.

Summer vacation in progress.

Scores of young people enjoying themselves on the Manhattan Beach.

A young girl was roaming the beach, looking around frantically…

The girl's name was Judith Maitlon, and she lived with her parents in LA, California… Manhattan, near the beach, to be exact.

Her parents called her by her birth name, Judith, but she preferred the less rigid form; Judy…

At a quick glance, she could've been mistaken for a very happy person. That was because, even at age 14, she knew how to keep current the façade of 'being happy.'

She was a great actor who knew how to hide her true feelings…

But Judy lived a double life.

On the one hand, she was Judith, the seemingly happy, cheerful and outgoing daughter of Professors Rudolph and Melissa Maitlon, the Scientists who owned the *MaitlonByTwo Research*

Center near the Hawthorne College Medical Center on Hawthorne Blvd... the scientists who appeared to care only for their work at the *MaitlonByTwo Research Center*, seemingly completely neglecting their only daughter in favor of their research work... the daughter who, subsequently, were one of the loneliest and unhappiest people in Manhattan...

On the other hand, she was Judy, called Judda by her more questionable, infamous acquaintances.

A frivolous, daring (delinquent, almost) student in her sophomore year, she took the lead in whichever bout of mischief or disruption could find its way into the confines of her 'Alma Mater,' the *Futures Academy* on *Wilshire Blvd, Beverly Hills.*

Judy was, indeed, a very unhappy person deep inside, and her bouts of misconduct were the result of that unhappiness, manifesting from deep down inside of her very soul. And this unhappiness also gave birth to her quick decision, acting on peer pressure one night, to try out the worst of all drugs, heroine... the fiercest 'dragon' of them all...

The fact that she'd already experimented with other drugs, made the decision about taking heroine quite a bit easier.

If she'd only left it at that, not returning for more, it would not have had the ultimate adverse effect on her life that it had. If it remained at one dose, the drug would've worked itself out of her system and the only really bad physical consequence would've been the 'low' after the 'high' of the drug.

But being Judy, she wanted to explore this new level of 'feeling high.'

Unfortunately, the euphoric heroine 'high' only lasts for about an hour, if that, and then the 'low' kicks in.

Some are lucky enough to experience this 'low' as being 'sleepy,' or 'drowsy.' They could easily fall asleep, and later wake up, wanting more of the 'dragon...'

Others experience it as 'feeling utterly depressed...' since ultimately, that is what heroine is... a depressant...

And it is that feeling of utter dark depression that is responsible for the fact that the heroine addict keeps wanting more and more of the drug and keeps returning to their supplier, time and time again... because they cannot handle the depression... and when the pain caused by withdrawal kicks in, it's even worse...

For Judy, it went from one dose to another, and another, and soon she'd found herself in the 'hell' called 'Heroine addiction...' the domain of the 'dragon.'

For the sake of this book, and privacy, I have changed her name, so Judy was not her real name.

Her place of residence as described above was also fictitious, as was the names and workplace of her parents...

Judy was perceived as blessed, living with her highly esteemed parents in such a beautiful and popular city...

...Los Angeles, the City of Angels...

Or was it...?

*****

Day by day, after school, Judy would walk along the beach with her friends... first to enjoy their company, but later in search of her 'dragon,' heroine.

She would walk the Manhattan Beach Pier, the trademark of Manhattan Beach, looking for someone to buy heroine from...

Usually, she would find her 'savior' in some peddler whose 'hell' it was to supply drugs to those who were addicted to the 'hell of drugs.' Should she find him on the beach, she'd buy her 'dragon,' then head home to 'shoot up...'

If not... then she would turn to the streets of Downtown, Manhattan to look for him there...

And there they all were, in abundance... on the streets... the mules, peddlers and users, strutting their stuff trying to cut their deals to either make a living, or to survive another day on a fix. Sometimes even both...

In such a Case, where she'd had to brave the streets, she'd head home quite a bit later, being at risk, then, to be caught by her parents in the process of 'shooting up...'

But she'd learned, over time, to avoid being caught.

She began to hide her gear where she'd used to hide her 'stash' when it was still only 'weed' that she'd had to worry about.

With the 'dragon,' she had no 'stash.' At fifty bucks a shot, she couldn't afford to keep 'stash.' She had to use her lunch money every day to buy her 'fix....'

*****

Because of some past bout of misconduct, the peddlers and mules were unofficially prohibited to walk on the pier, or stroll along the beach... the users were welcome, as long as they behaved themselves... and as long as they went elsewhere to get their 'dragon...'

At some stage, the prohibition was extended to the downtown areas. Later, the state began to crack down hard on the mules, the peddlers and even the users...

Subsequently, prospects for selling- or buying the drugs on the beach, the pier or even the streets of Downtown, Manhattan, became less and less, as more and more users (mostly members of the 'wealthy,' the more 'well-to-do' faction of Society), had bought into the 'fashion' of having their daily fix (or two)... or their week's or month's supply of whichever of the several available 'dragons' they'd served, delivered to their homes. Whether their 'dragon' was called heroine, or cocaine, or ecstasy... or merely cannabis or hash... the wealthy people had no problem acquiring their drug (or drugs - yes, some of them used more than one), since they had their regular suppliers, who always supplied the 'best quality' to the 'best people.'

They would serve cocaine (or coke, crack, or powder, as it's sometimes called) on their parties like other people would serve snacks and drinks... and they'd use it as a daily crutch... a 'crutch,' because the only time that they were feeling 'normal,' or at least 'as normal as possible,' was when they were under the influence... since cocaine is a stimulant and they constantly had to be under its influence in order to avoid the feeling of utter depression following the short-lived 'high... or, in severe Maitlons, to prevent heart failure, which was a usual side effect of cocaine... because it was a stimulant...

The people who supplied drugs to the 'yuppies,' as someone had once dubbed the 'wealthy clique,' didn't mind the change in routine since they were the 'lucky' ones... the ones that had no problem getting rid of their 'stuff.' They didn't have to walk up and down in the streets of Downtown, Manhattan or on the Manhattan Beach Pier anymore. They could now simply 'sit back' and wait for the phone to ring, and then do their rounds, making certain that they delivered the 'dragon' on time...

However, the street vendors, the so-called 'peddlers' that kept supplying drugs to the street junkies, lost the greatest part of their income, since the 'wealthy clique' were those people in Society that had no problem paying for the 'good stuff.' And these street vendors were in the unfortunate position of not being able to join the 'lucky ones,' since, for whatever reason, they were kind of 'banned' from Society...

The street junkies, users who basically had nothing left to lose, began to care less and less that their smack or coke was being laced with either substitutes such as Fentanyl or Mandrax in the Case of heroine... or Ketamine or Phencyclidine (PCP) in the Case of cocaine...

Ruthless pushers even turned to so-called 'fillers' to increase the volume of whichever drugs they'd peddled...

NOTE: MIXING DRUGS CAN BE EXTREMELY DANGEROUS, EVEN IF PURE SUBSTANCES ARE MIXED TOGETHER.

ONE OF THE MOST DANGEROUS DRUG MIXTURES IS A 'SPEEDBALL,' WHICH IS WHAT A MIXTURE OF HEROINE AND COCAINE IS CALLED.

USING A 'SPEEDBALL' CAN BE LETHAL, SINCE IT IS A COMBINATION OF A STIMULANT AND A DEPRESSANT. THE ONE DOES NOT CANCEL OUT THE EFFECT OF THE OTHER, RATHER, THE TWO DRUGS WORK IN CONJUNCTION WITH EACH OTHER IN SUCH A WAY THAT THE ONE ACTUALLY INCREASES THE ADVERSE EFFECTS OF THE OTHER... AND VICE VERSA.

BECAUSE A COCAINE HIGH ONLY LASTS ABOUT AN HOUR, AND THE USER THEN EXPERIENCES DEPRESSION, SLUGGISHNESS, AND AN EXTREME LOW, THE USER OF A 'SPEEDBALL' CAN DIE WHEN THE STIMULATING EFFECT OF COCAINE TURNS INTO A DEPRESSING LOW AND THE DEPRESSING EFFECT OF HEROINE, WHICH NATURALLY IS A DEPRESSANT, KICKS IN. HEROINE CAN SIGNIFICANTLY INCREASE THE DEPRESSING EFFECT CAUSED BY THE 'ABSENCE OF COCAINE.' THE DOUBLE EFFECT OF HEROINE AND COCAINE SLOWS DOWN THE BREATHING, HEART RATE AND BLOOD PRESSURE OF THE USER TO THE EXTENT THAT THE LUNGS AND HEART OF THE USER CAN STOP, CAUSING DEATH...

MERELY MIXING THE DRUGS TOGETHER IS ALREADY BAD ENOUGH, BUT WHEN THE PUSHER IS DESPERATE TO TRY AND MAKE A LIVING AND THEN MIX TOGETHER ANYTHING THAT LOOKS LIKE THE DRUG THAT HE OR SHE IS TRYING TO PUSH, THE RESULT CAN BE LETHAL. IT HAD BEEN RECORDED THAT EVEN POISONOUS SUBSTANCES SUCH AS RAT POISON AND ARSENIC HAD BEEN FOUND IN PACKETS OF DRUGS THAT WERE CONFISCATED BY THE POLICE.

More and more users began to either land in hospital or to die as a result of using bad quality drugs. And there was also the problem of users dying of an overdose, because the volume of their drugs was increased by means of adding harmless substances such as icing sugar, corn starch or milk powder, forcing the user to buy more and more of their drug to get the same effect. And when you have to do that, you can never be sure of how much of the actual drug is in the mixture.

This problem of drug mixtures had caused more trouble than the use of one single drug, but the down and out users who had nowhere else to get their daily fix from, kept returning for more because to them, the alternative of not getting their daily fix was far worse.

Now Judy, as it were, did fall in the 'wealthy' category, but her parents weren't drug users, so Judy wasn't so lucky. She still had to get her 'dragon,' but now she had to turn to peddlers on the street. And having to use her lunch money, her system was weakened because she didn't eat at all during the day.

On this particular summer day, Judy became part of statistics... she became one of the unfortunate users who nearly died of an overdose because of watered down drugs... she'd shot up two doses of filler-laced heroine bought from a 'cheap' dealer and got more than she'd bargained for...

No wonder then that Judy, who at least had some sense, when she was discharged from hospital, decided to try and kick the habit. And she would've succeeded, had it not been for a devil worse than the heroine drug. A devil called 'scientific deceits...' or more aptly put, 'lies in the name of science.'

Chapter 2 – Getting Clean

Monday, July 27th, 1987

Judy's parents, after learning about her problem with drugs, were devastated... not because they actually cared about her, but because of their shattered reputation, should their friends and colleagues find out...

*****

7 pm

Judy had just arrived back home after escaping from the rehab center, and the Maitlon family were discussing Judy's drug addiction over dinner.

Judy was not very co-operative... just listening, keeping quiet...

"Judith," said Professor Rudolph Maitlon, "You have two options..."

Judy rolled her eyes...

"Choose now..." continued her father. "Either you go back to the rehabilitation center, or we bring someone, a nurse, from the research center to come and live in here for the next four weeks to take care of you while you detox."

"Why should I choose either?" retaliated Judy. "Why can't I just stay upstairs in my room and go 'cold turkey?'"

"It's the 'cold turkey' aspect of it that I'm concerned about." Said Professor Rudolph Maitlon. "Have you ever seen someone go 'cold turkey' when on heroine?"

"No, I didn't." Admitted Judy. "But I did see you and Mom doing the detox thing when you quit coffee. That was pretty bad, given the headaches and all. But I could do that. Isn't the heroine 'cold turkey' basically the same?"

"Not even remotely the same." Replied Professor Maitlon. "The withdrawal symptoms for heroine are the worst withdrawal symptoms ever. Multiply the effects of caffeine withdrawal by 10000."

"That's why we're suggesting that you allow a nurse to come and take care of you for the next four weeks." Explained Professor Melissa Maitlon. "Otherwise, you will have to go back to the rehabilitation center. As simple as that…"

Judy shrugged.

"Okay, let's try the nurse." Agreed Judy. "Much rather that than the fricking rehab…"

"So it's settled then." Declared her father. "We will bring in the nurse tomorrow."

Judy went to her bedroom, closed the door behind her and took out the packet of heroine that she'd bought earlier.

She stared at it for a while, then put it in her bed table drawer.

'May as well start trying the detox thing,' she thought…

Chapter 3 - Shauna

Tuesday, July 28th, 1987

9 am

The next morning the nurse, Shauna, arrived. Professor Rudolph Maitlon had already left for work.

Professor Melissa Maitlon introduced Shauna to Judy, and then also left for work.

"Hi Judith," said Shauna. "I hope…

Judy interrupted her…

"Judy!" she said brusquely. "My name is Judy! I don't know why my parents keep calling me by my stupid birth name…"

Shauna nodded.

"Okay," she said. "Judy then. Now where was I? Oh yeah! I hope we can do this together without any hiccups."

'Hiccups?' thought Judy. 'The fact that you're here is already one mammoth 'hiccup.' And obviously, your reason for being here is another mammoth hiccup…'

But as always, Judy kept any thoughts to herself that could cause her any trouble…

'Okay,' thought Shauna, sizing Judy up. 'So you're not very talkative. We'll see for how long you keep this up, young lady…'

She looked at Judy sternly, but with a glint of empathy in her eyes.

"Let's just make it very clear right from the very beginning." Declared Shauna. 'I am being paid by your parents, and am here to follow instructions… your parents' instructions, not yours… is that clear?"

Judy nodded, and then sulked. When she thought nobody was looking, she stealthily slipped the tiny packet from the night before into her jean pocket…

Shauna moved into the spare bedroom, which was next to Judy's bedroom, then went back to the kitchen, where Judy was preparing some bacon and eggs for herself.

Judy looked up when Shauna entered the kitchen.

"You may prepare yourself some breakfast if you wish, Shauna." Said Judy. "Same goes for lunch and all other meals. Make yourself some tea whenever you feel like it…"

"Thank you, Judy," replied Shauna. "I will keep that in mind. Now, could I please have that dose of heroine that I saw you slip into your pocket just now?"

"But…" protested Judy. "I don't have any…"

But Shauna interrupted her…

"Judy," said Shauna. "I'm a nurse. I know the withdrawal symptoms, and I know how long it usually takes before it kicks in… and you haven't shown any of those symptoms yet… which means that you probably still have heroine on you. Now let me have it, please…"

"But I don't…" began Judy, but Shauna interrupted her again…

"Judy," she said, holding out her hand. "I don't want to do this the hard way. Give me that packet please…!"

Judy stared at Shauna, then took the heroine out of her pocket, pouting. She handed it over to Shauna, who washed it down the sink.

Judy kept staring at Shauna, and if looks could kill, Shauna would've been a gonner…

"That was my last packet," said Judy tearfully. "It cost me quite a bit and I wanted to hang on to it to help me through the withdrawal…"

"It wouldn't have helped you at all, believe me," explained Shauna. "If anything, it would've made matters worse. I have got some meds that will make the load a bit lighter. It's called Methadone. When you need it, I will administer it..."

Judy suddenly didn't want to be in Shauna's presence anymore. She turned around and ran to her bedroom. She slammed the door closed and locked herself in.

She fell on her bed and sulked for a little while, then fell asleep.

*****

11 am

Judy woke up. She had a throbbing headache and the muscles in her neck, back and shoulders were aching badly...

'Dammit!' she thought, 'this gets any worse, it's gonna kill me!"

She went to the kitchen and made herself a cup of coffee. She took two bread rolls from the bread bin, and packed them with all kinds of fillings, including cheese, ham, gherkins and tomato, topping the combo with mayonnaise.

She took two more bread rolls and spread them thick with peanut butter and apricot jelly.

Finally, she took two cans of soda from the fridge.

'I think this should do it for now,' she thought. 'I don't want to leave that room for the next two days."

After eating a bread roll and drinking the coffee, she took the rest of the food and the sodas to her bedroom and put it on her bed table. Then she went to Shauna's bedroom and knocked.

"Come in!" said Shauna.

Shauna looked pleasantly surprised to see Judy.

"Hi Judy," she said. "How are you doing?"

"Hi Shauna. Not too wonderful," replied Judy. "I'm sorry about the tantrum..."

"No problem, Judy," replied Shauna, smiling sympathetically. "Tantrums are perfectly normal for someone in your position..."

'Stop patronizing me!' thought Judy, but once again kept her thoughts to herself.

"Thank you for understanding, Shauna." She said. "I think the withdrawal symptoms are beginning."

"Okay, just remain calm," said Shauna. "And shout if you need me to give you something to help you through it."

"Okay will do," replied Judy. "But I'm actually just letting you know that I'm going to lie down. I don't really have anything else to do. And I don't need anything called 'Methadone' to help me through it. I might as well just lie down until it's over..."

"I mean it, Judy," said Shauna. "You have to go through withdrawal and detox, but the meds I can give you will ease the pain. The withdrawal will be much less uncomfortable."

"Thanks Shauna," replied Judy. "I'll think about it."

She turned around and went to her bedroom. She closed the door and locked it.

"This is gonna suck!" she said to nobody in particular. "But the stuff that's for sale on the street, lately, will kill a horse, let alone a human being with a weakened immune system... with things being the way that they are at the moment, I will cause my own death if I don't do this. I've made a decision, and I'm going through with it, come hell or high water. But sure as hell, if I'm gonna go 'cold turkey,' it will be without some 'nurse' who keeps telling me what to do. I'm not leaving my bedroom for the next 2 days, at least. At the end of it, I want to be clean..."

Judy took a peanut butter and jelly bread roll and eats it. Then she finished a can of soda. She looked at the two remaining rolls and took one...

'Might as well eat before I die,' she thought. 'I'd rather die with a full stomach than die hungry...'

She finished both remaining rolls.

Suddenly, she got a hot flush.

The air conditioner was on and freezing, yet somehow Judy felt as though she was boiling from the inside out, perspiring profusely. She felt hot to the bone...

Her bones began throbbing and her eyes began to water overwhelmingly. Judy realized that she was really feeling seriously sick.

'Shit!' She thought. "It really is starting..."

It had only been approximately twenty hours since Judy had her last fix, and she already felt terrible. She slowly lay down on her bed and tried to sleep, but the symptoms grew worse. She tried to focus on something else. Eventually, she fell into a state of semi-delirium...

Chapter 4 – Hard Detox

Tuesday, July 28th, 1987

3 pm

Judy screamed herself awake. Her entire body was convulsing and in extreme pain. She tried to sit up, but couldn't...

There was a knock on her bedroom door...

"Judy," came Shauna's concerned voice, "If you can stand up and get to the door in any way, unlock it so that I can administer some Methadone for the pain..."

Judy's chilling scream split the air again...

"Judy can you hear me?" Shauna wanted to know.

Shauna listened intently. All she could hear was Judy sobbing and intermittently groaning.

"Judy," inquired Shauna, "Is there a spare key to your bedroom. I want to come in and administer some Methadone. I will inject it, so you won't have to swallow..."

Sobbing, then a chilling scream...

"Holy Shit, this is hell!" cried Judy. "I have died and was sent to hell...!"

"Judy," tried Shauna again, "The withdrawal is potentially fatal. I need to get into your room so that I can help you..."

She attempted a soft knock on the door.

The response was a spine-chilling scream and then a gagging sound. Obviously, Judy was nauseous. She would need to visit the bathroom soon...

"Judy," tried Shauna. "Do you need to go to the bathroom?"

Silence, then the sound of a toilet flushing.

'Thank goodness,' thought Shauna. *'She has her own bathroom...'*

Shauna turned around and went to the kitchen to make herself a cup of coffee. She returned and knocked on Judy's bedroom door again.

"Judy," she said. "Just call if you need me. I'll be next door in my bedroom…"

No answer, but Shauna could hear Judy groaning loudly. Shauna went to her bedroom to drink her coffee. Obviously, that was where she would spend the rest of the afternoon and probably the entire night as well…

After a while, all was quiet again.

'Sounds like she's passed out from the pain,' thought Shauna.

She went to the kitchen to make herself a cup of tea.

'This should be fine for now,' she thought as she took a few cookies from a serving tray and went to her bedroom. 'Don't want to be out of earshot when she wakes up again…!'

*****

6 pm

Wave upon wave of excruciating pain surged through Judy's body as she screamed herself awake again.

"Shit! Shit! Shit!" she yelled as she tried to get up. "Gotta get to the bathroom NOW!"

She eventually succeeded getting up and then she moved to the bathroom.

She only made it halfway across when her torso contracted and she spilled her stomach's entire contents all over her floor rug… her stomach continued contracting intermittently for the next 5 minutes.

She grabbed a towel from her wardrobe and tried to wipe up as much of the mess from the rug as she was able to under the circumstances.

Furious, she flung the towel in a corner of the bedroom.

She looked at the second can of soda she didn't drink before, shook her hurting head and went to the bathroom to drink some water.

The water had barely reached her stomach, before it came out immediately. She rinsed out her mouth and began to move back to her bedroom.

She'd barely reached the door when her stomach began to growl. She made the toilet just in time.

Back on her bed, she tried to sleep, but symptom after symptom caused her to scream every few seconds.

"This is fricking ridiculous!" She yelled at nobody in particular. "When the hell will it end?! I'm totally spent already!"

The flash of her bedroom light coming on almost blinded her. She couldn't focus to see who'd entered her bedroom...

"Wtf!?" she yelled. "Who gave you permission to come in here!? Where did you get the fricking key, anyway!? This is *my* fricking bedroom! *My* domain! Get out, for heaven's sake!"

"Calm down, Judith," said her mother. "I'd used the key on my keyring and I came in to see if you were okay..."

"Get... out!" yelled Judy. "And for heaven's sake, turn off that light! It's driving me crazy...!"

"Judith," said her mother. "I am going to undress you and give you a bath and then dress you in pajamas and put you to bed. You look and smell horrendous..."

"No!" yelled Judy. "Get out!"

"Not until you've been cleaned up," replied Professor Melissa Maitlon. "If you don't want me to do that, I'll call Shauna to do it instead. Also, I've taken your bedroom key to keep you from locking yourself in again. You can have it back when you're though all this. Things need to be done around here, and I'm paying for the meds that you so deftly refuse..."

If looks could kill, Professor Melissa Maitlon would've been dead… But Judy kept quiet and allowed her mother to clean her up.

With Judy back in bed, Professor Maitlon turned to leave the room…

"Oh! Before I forget," she said, as she put a pair of flat-heeled slippers next to the bed. "Wear these when you need to get to the bathroom. Those high-heeled things that you've probably slept with all day will be a hindrance when you need to get there fast…"

Professor Maitlon left the room…

Shauna entered the room and pulled out a syringe. She took a hypodermic needle from a packet and attached it to the syringe. Then she pulled some Methadone into the syringe.

"Judy," she said. "This will only take a second and it will make you feel much better. It's Methadone. It will relieve the pain that accompanies the withdrawal symptoms…"

Judy could do nothing but look on while Shauna injected her. She had no strength for anything else…

She watched attentively as Shauna injected the Methadone. Her stomach contracted automatically just by looking at it.

Judy's palms began to sweat and she instantaneously felt as though she might be on her way to the bathroom again. Her skin felt like thousands of insects were crawling under it and her legs felt weak and restless.

Then Judy felt her body relax as the Methadone began to work its magic. Before long, she was fast asleep…

Shauna took the opportunity to take out the soiled rug and towel to put it in the washing machine, and clean up whatever else needed cleaning…

*****

Wednesday, July 29th, 1987

9 am

"Good morning Judy," she heard Shauna's voice. "How are you feeling?"

"Like shit!" replied Judy.

"C'mon, we gotta take some blood samples to determine the heroine content in your body, and whether heroine is all that was in your last dose…"

"Is that necessary?" Judy demanded. "I hate these needles that you keep sticking into me…"

"And what makes them any different from the ones you'd used to shoot up your drugs?" Shauna wanted to know.

"Well," replied Judy. "I handle my own needles and I don't like the fact that you're handling these…"

"These tests are necessary, Judy." Explained Shauna. "Without them, we won't know exactly when all traces of the drug had left your body."

Judy decided to work with Shauna on this.

She nodded.

Before long, her blood samples were taken and she was given a bathroom scale to stand on so that Shauna could record her weight. Shauna measured Judy at the same time to record her height…

Next, her blood pressure was taken and recorded.

Finally, Judy got another shot of Methadone…

"Well there you go!" said Shauna. "All done! From now on, I will just monitor you twice a day to make sure that you have a safe detox, and give you some Methadone, if necessary."

"Why can't you just leave the Methadone on the bed table and leave me alone so that I can administer it myself?"

"Because," explained Shauna, "Methadone is an opiate. It can be addictive too. It is used to ease the pain, because that is what opiates do. They are pain killers…"

'This is going to fricking suck.' Thought Judy again before she fell asleep once again...

*****

But before long, Shauna had won Judy over completely. The two of them were getting on well together, and Judy was well on her way to recovery...

Chapter 5 – Reintroduced and Recaptured

Four Weeks Later

Monday, August 31st, 1987

9 am

Judy had completed her detox, and was resting and recovering at home before having to return to school a week and a half later.

One day, when Judy was down and out, and emotionally especially vulnerable after her recent 'detox' experience, and terribly depressed because her parents didn't seem to care about her, and with Shauna having had successfully completed her task and having left for home just the previous day to resume her job at the *MaitlonByTwo Research Center*... the 'devil' came along and knocked on Judy's door.

He came in the form of a pusher that used to supply heroine to Judy on the streets, but had decided to serve the 'wealthy,' 'well-to-do' faction of Society...

...and he had brought the 'dragon' with him...

His actual name was Bart. His nickname, which was the name that Judy knew him by, was HeroBart... 'Hero' being an indication of his 'profession,' or 'trade.'

With Shauna not being there for her anymore, Judy was particularly vulnerable. Obviously, HeroBart must have watched Judy's home, and must have seen Shauna's taxi leave... And, as was the case with most all of the pushers at the time, it was his clear intention, right then, to get Judy 'hooked' again... which was the reason why he'd brought the 'dragon' along...

At first, Judy didn't recognize him when she opened her door to him.

"Yes?" said Judy. "Can I help you?"

"Hey Judda," replied HeroBart. "You look terrible!"

"I feel terrible!" responded Judy. "Just been through a horrible four weeks. But I'm rested and on my way to recovery..."

He nodded knowingly...

"case of 'super-flu?'" he asked, just to make light conversation. The practice of getting rid of drugs by kicking the habit by means of going 'cold turkey' was sometimes referred to as 'super-flu.'

"Yes," she confirmed, looking down. She couldn't look him in the eye since she wasn't exactly proud of having had to rid herself of an illegal substance...

"You don't recognize me?" he wanted to know, frowning.

Then Judy looked at HeroBart more closely and finally recognized him.

"Okay," she said, "now I do recognize you. You're HeroBart, whom I used to buy heroine from. Why did you come here?"

"Judda..." he said in a soothing tone of voice. "I just came to find out if you needed anything..."

She immediately recognized the word 'anything' as meaning 'heroine.'

"No," she said abruptly, "I'm done with that now. I think you'd better leave..."

But her eyes kept following the small packet he held in his hand, flaunting it, making sure that she was completely aware of it.

"This is genuine stuff, Judda," he assured her. "I don't sell anything that's been 'doctored' with other stuff. You know that, don't you?"

She nodded.

"Yes," she replied. "I know that. But I told you I'm done. Could you please leave now, before I fall for the temptation and go for it...?"

"Okay," he said. "But I'll leave it here in case you change your mind..."

He left the packet on her doorstep, and left.

Judy closed the door, leaving the packet where it was, but immediately opened it again, picking it up and taking it inside with the intention of throwing it away.

'Don't want my parents to see it,' she thought...

At that moment, her phone rang... it was Professor Melissa Maitlon...

"Hi Judith,' she greeted as Judy answered the call. "How are you doing with Shauna not there anymore?"

"I'm fine Mom." Replied Judy. "How are you?"

"I'm fine Judith," replied her Mom. "But you're the one I'm really concerned about. Just making sure you're not taking drugs again now that Shauna has left..."

"No real 'how are you' for the of ME Mom?" Judy wanted to know. "I have feelings and a soul too, you know? But don't worry, I'm fine. Not taking drugs again..."

"Then that's fine, Judith." Said Professor Maitlon. "See you at home tonight, then..."

She hung up...

Judy began to cry softly.

"She really does not care about me at all," she sobbed.

She looked at the packet in her hand for a full minute... then made a quick, disastrous, decision... and before the end of the day, Judy Maitlon was addicted to the 'dragon' again...

*****

The next morning

HeroBart was back with another 'free' packet.

And Judy couldn't wait to shoot it up and experience the familiar feeling of the drug invading her body. That amazing high-spirited feeling that always used to give her 'go...' at least until the euphoric high wore off...

And she giggled...

Too bad that feeling lasted only a few minutes... not even as long as the 'high' you'd get when sniffing coke...

Bart stayed a while, talking to Judy to see if he could 'score.'

He coerced her into removing her clothes... coerced her into letting him have his way with her...

And then he left, with a promise that he'd be back the next day.

At age 15, Judy was not a virgin anymore...

She felt particularly depressed. She also felt dirty...

'How could I have allowed that?' she thought. 'He's not even particularly attractive.

Judy took a shower, trying to wash away the feeling of filth that was clinging to her, but to no avail...

*****

The next day

Bart stayed away on purpose the next day, but the morning after that, he was back again... and this time, the packet carried a price...

Judy was beside herself, wanting a 'fix' so badly that she was prepared to let him have his way with her again. But Bart was rigid. He insisted on being paid... in cash...

"Sorry, Judda." He said. "This one is fifty bucks..."

Judy almost fainted. She had no money with her, since her pocket money was suspended until she would be able to confidently carry cash without wanting to spend it on a 'fix...'

"Bart, please!" she wailed. "Just this one more time..."

"I don't know Girl," he said. "Remember, I need to make a living too..."

He turned and left, leaving her in dire straits...

She just stood there, wondering what she was going to do if she had to do the 'cold turkey' thing again...

And then, Bart returned...

Chapter 6 – Intimidation and Duress

Tuesday, September 1ˢᵗ, 1987

12.30 pm

"I think I left my cap here," Bart explained.

He looked around, saw the cap, took it, and turned to leave..

"I thought you were my friend, Bart." Wailed Judy. "I would never be able to pay that kind of money for one fix. It's ten times what you've charged before…"

"Come now, Judda," said Bart, smirking. "This stuff is much better and a lot purer than the stuff I used to sell before. Giving it to you for free, or even at the old price, would be financial suicide."

"But I thought we were friends, Bart." Replied Judy. "Please give it to me at the old price, just this once?"

He looked at her and recognized the symptoms of withdrawal. And he knew that she wouldn't even be able to buy the drug at the old price…

'I know I have her on tow again,' he thought, 'whether I sell her the stuff, or give it to her for free. But she's only had two doses so far, so she might be able to break free again. Perhaps only this one more time…'

He made a quick decision…

"Okay Honey," he said, holding out a packet towards her. "Just this one more time, it's yours for free. But tomorrow, you'll have to pay for your fix…"

"Oh! Thank you Bart!" she exclaimed, crying. "You're a true friend! You won't regret this, you'll see!"

"No problem, Sweetie," he said. "We have each other's backs…"

But in his mind, he was already planning his next move. And his next move was as evil as they come…

"I'll be back again tomorrow," he said.

But she was already shooting up the drug, not even hearing his words. And he silently laughed at her...

'Hell!' he thought with a tinge of bitterness in his mind, 'Doesn't she know that there's no such thing as 'true friendship' in this corrupt and filthy lifestyle that we have both chosen as our master...?'

*****

The next morning

The next day when he laid his eyes on her, he knew with complete certainty that Judy was his. He would be able to coerce her into anything he wanted, since she needed nothing more than she needed the drug... and she couldn't pay for it with money, since she had none...

"Bart?" she pleaded, "Just this once more?"

But he was even more rigid than the previous time. He put the packet back in his pocket, turned around and began to walk away.

"Bart!" she wailed. "Please, I'll do anything..!"

He stopped in mid-stride...

Then he turned back, facing her again.

"Anything?" he wanted to know.

"Anything!" She replied, tears streaking her hollow cheeks...

"Even if it's illegal?" he asked.

"Anything, Bart!" she assured him, looking at him with pleading eyes.

Bart just stared at her, shaking his head.

"I don't know, Sweetheart," he said, wincing at the fact that he was actually calling her 'Sweetheart...'

"Anything Bart!" she pleaded again, "Anything… I've got to have that packet…!"

"Okay," he said as he handed her the packet. "Let's go inside. Shoot this up and then we'll talk…"

They closed the door behind them, and went to her bedroom. She shot up the heroine and then they sat down on her bed, facing each other.

"Okay," he said, smiling. "Now that you're feeling better and I have your attention, here's the thing. I am working for a group of scientists who are in the process of developing a method of altering human DNA. They will change the genetic structure of a person in such a way as to enhance every talent of such a person. They are aiming at improving the genome of the human race. They need two groups of subjects to experiment on."

"What type of 'enhancement?" Judy wanted to know. "It sounds like something that could improve your life…?"

"In a sense, yes," lied the devil, who is, after all, the father of lies…

"Explain?" said Judy.

"Okay," explained Bart. "With the first group, they will experiment on the subject in order to enhance the DNA of the person. This group needs to be physically and mentally completely fit, and healthy and without blemish. They are the donors of the enhanced DNA…"

"And the second group?" inquired Judy.

"The second group," continued Bart, "will be people who want certain talents, or something that they think they desperately need in their lives and who want to be 'enhanced' in a way. In other words, the first group will be the guinea pigs so that the other group can receive what they want… People from both groups will be individuals who won't mind being treated with stuff that haven't been approved by the FDA yet…"

Horrified, Judy just stared at him…

"Continue?" she requested, hoping that he would say something that would make his explanation sound less senseless and more ethical...

"Obviously," continued Bart, "both groups of people will be handsomely rewarded for participating...

"Rewarded"? Inquired Judy. "How?"

"Well," replied Bart. "We will offer them each $1 Million to participate. As assurance, should a subject die, we will undertake to pay the money over to his or her next of kin..."

"Die?!" interjected Judy. "I see, and where do I fit into this picture? What does this have to do with me, Bart? I'm not exactly what you would call a 'healthy person without blemish,' so they won't be able to test any of this so-called 'DNA enhancement therapy' on me..."

"Yes I know that." He confirmed. "But this is a very lucrative business, albeit illegal. What I want you to do, is to coax young, healthy people who need money to agree to being experimented on, in return for a new life."

"O-o-okay...' responded Judy. "And what about the other group? How do *they* fit into the picture?"

"Well," replied Bart. "Obviously, this group will be the source of the DNA that the other group will receive to give them the lives that they want..."

"And what happens if any of this 'therapy' backfires when used on someone and it's not a success?" Judy wanted to know. "Will they survive and be released back into Society and be able to carry on with their lives"?

"So far," replied Bart, "only one person had been released back into Society after the treatment failed. He had disappeared. Nobody knows where he is at the moment..."

"Why would he choose to 'disappear,' as you've just called it?" Judy demands...

"Well, actually," explained Bart, "he turned out not to be quite the same person. His original DNA structure was … uhm… altered… one of the chromosomes got messed up, and, as I said, he'll never be quite the same ever again…"

Chapter 7 – Changing the 'Dragon'

"No!" exclaimed Judy. "How could you?! So this person will be a freak for the rest of his life?"

"Unfortunately, yes." Admitted Bart. "And unfortunately, this does happen from time to time... Let's just call it 'collateral damage...'"

"What do you mean... from time to time?" demanded Judy, but she slowly began to realize the horrible truth... "And how could you be so... cold and heartless as to call it 'collateral damage?' Aren't these human beings we are talking about?!"

"Judda," replied Bart. "The fact of the matter is that he did not die. He survived. Some of the others didn't. But the gene therapy caused him to suddenly start growing again. And he grew out of proportion. He is now over eight feet tall. But his brain capacity had shrunk..."

Judy stared at Bart in horror. She shook her head.

"I don't think I can do that, Bart." She said. "It's not only illegal, it's also immoral. The answer is 'no,' and that's final!"

"Think carefully, Judy," replied Bart. "Are you absolutely certain about this?"

"Absolutely!" confirmed Judy. "I cannot take part in a project that could mean the destruction of someone's life... could ultimately mean the destruction of human life as we know it. I cannot begin to fathom the kind of 'reality' that that poor man now has to live with. And who knows for how long? Who knows how long he will have to live with that still? Who's to say that he will die soon? That his DNA hasn't been altered to the extent that he will live much longer than a human usually does? As I said, the answer is 'no,' and that's final."

"Okay," he replied. "But before I go, you need to pay me."

"Pay you?" she said.

"Yes," he replied, holding out his hand. "You owe me some money for the heroine ... every packet that you got from me since the beginning of the week..."

"But," she said. "I thought it was a gift...?"

"Yes," he replied, "a conditional gift. You've agreed to work with me and you went back on your word. So pay up, please!"

"Bart?" Judy now practically begged him for mercy. "I honestly don't know where I'll get that amount of money to pay you!"

"Your problem, Girl!" he replied.

"Bart, please!" begged Judy

But Bart was relentless.

"As I said, girl," he repeated. "You've agreed to work with me and you went back on your word. So pay up, please!"

Judy made a quick decision...

'I'm not going to stand for this nonsense...' she thought. "I'll go to the police and tell them..."

"Can you give me until tomorrow?" she wanted to know. "I'll try and find the money. I think I can borrow it from my mom."

But as she said it, she already realized that she had a big problem. If she went to the police, she'd be locked up for drug abuse... and Bart would be in jail, so he wouldn't be able to supply her drugs...

"Okay until tomorrow then," replied Bart.

He smirked as he turned around and walked away. He knew she wouldn't be able to get the money. He also knew that he solidly had her on a string...

And Judy knew it would be impossible to find the money. Her mother would never give her the money, since she would know right away that it would be used to pay for drugs. As it was, Professor Melissa Maitlon wouldn't even allow her daughter back into the house unless she'd agreed to let Shauna help her detox.

'If Mom had to find out I'm back on 'smack,' thought Judy, 'I'll be out on the street, for sure… As it is, Dad had to convince her to let me stay in the first place…

Bart stayed away the next day.

Judy began to experience withdrawal symptoms again, and she began to panic…

Friday, September 4th, 1987

12.30 pm

When Bart arrived at her door the day after that, Judy was as tame as a lamb, and ready to negotiate.

Bart once again gave her a dose of heroine, and after she got her 'fix,' they talked about the DNA manipulation venture again.

This time, Judy was a lot more agreeable.

"But where would I find these people?" she wanted to know. "I've never done something like this before."

"Don't worry, Sweetie," replied Bart. "I will teach you the ropes before I let you go out on your own."

"Okay," she agreed. "When will you teach me?"

"How about tomorrow?" he wanted to know. "Would that suit you?"

She nodded.

"Okay," said Bart. "See you tomorrow then."

He turned to walk away, but then turned back.

"Just to show you that I care," he said as he handed her another dose. "Shoot this up tomorrow, before I come. I'll be here at 12 noon…"

"Okay." She agreed. "Thank you Bart. I'll see you tomorrow."

Saturday, September 5th, 1987

The next day, Bart was at her door at 11 am.

"Got your 'fix?'" he wanted to know.

She nodded.

Then he gave her another package and urged her to take it with her.

"That's just in case we return late," he explained. "I don't want you to get withdrawal symptoms while we're out in the field…"

"Field?" she wanted to know.

"Oh, that's just jargon." He explained. "It's slang for whichever place you choose to work at."

Judy winced at Bart's choice of words. Who'd have ever thought that someday, destroying human life would be considered 'work…?'

At exactly 12 noon, they left her home and he took her to Manhattan Beach.

"Does this seem familiar to you?" he asked.

She nodded.

"Yes," she said. "I remember a time when I walked this pier and this shoreline every day of my life, looking for someone to buy heroine from…"

"That's right," he said. "But from now on, you will browse the beach from the other perspective… the perspective not of a user, but of a supplier, albeit a supplier of a different kind of 'merchandize…'"

"But I'm still a user… of drugs, that is," she said.

"Yes." He admitted. "But you just bring your part, and you will never have to buy your 'fix,' ever again."

"How?" she wanted to know.

Well," he explained. "Part of the perks of your new job will be a free fix, every day, for life…"

"Completely free?" she asked.

She wanted that confirmation, so that she could make a final decision about the DNA manipulation thing.

And he gave her the confirmation she needed.

"Yes,' he replied. "Completely free."

The final bit of doubt within her heart melted away and dissipated in the hot Californian sun… Judy had been ensnared…

What Judy didn't realise, was that she was in the process of exchanging one 'dragon' for another. And the new 'dragon' was far worse than the existing one…

She also didn't know that Bart had laced the last two doses of heroine he'd given her with cocaine, causing her to shoot up a 'speedball' each time… she wouldn't be able to kick the habit so easily this time…

*****

"I have a little surprise for you." Said Bart.

To Judy, that sounded a bit sinister, but she followed him anyway. A few minutes later, she followed him into a small apartment only a few yards from the beach.

"Part of your perks for working for me." He explained. "And it's furnished, so you won't have to bring anything along. We can just pick up your clothes and other personal belongings."

To Judy, that was a solution. After her latest conversation with her mother, she'd already decided to leave. Bart had given her the means.

They went to pick up everything that she really wanted to take with her and she moved into her new apartment.

Chapter 8 – Speedball Complications

One year later

Saturday, September 10th, 1988

Bart strolled over to the Manhattan Beach Pier and assumed his usual position.

Judy sat down on a beach chair, under a beach umbrella.

She was wearing her sunglasses, hiding behind them, covertly looking at each and every person strolling on the beach. Any stranger looking at her may have mistaken her for a happy, wealthy person just killing some time while enjoying the Californian summer sun…

But such a person would've been sorely mistaken, for less than fifty yards away, on the Manhattan Beach Pier, Bart was standing, also supposedly covertly looking for prospective clients as well as prospective guinea pigs. But most of all, he was checking on Judy, making sure that she didn't 'step out of line.'

'Sometimes,' he thought, 'she really concerns me. I know I should've stopped the speedballs by now, but her kicking the habit almost entirely by means of 'cold turkey' concerns me. Mentally, she is a lot stronger than she thinks she is…'

For the time being, Judy had only been recruiting potential clients and identifying guinea pigs for Bart to recruit. According to Bart, she didn't have to deal with the guinea pigs, since they went directly to the scientist that prepared the patients and performed the procedures.

She saw a motley horde of people, but she couldn't really see whether they looked like prospective 'clients,' or potential 'guinea pigs.' She wouldn't admit this to herself, but that was because her eyesight was blurry… she'd been experiencing this for about a week now…

Judy got up and began to walk towards Bart, but stopped in mid-stride, feeling dizzy. It was like she suddenly couldn't put one foot in front of another, and she could hardly stand on her feet anymore...

Someone touched her shoulder. She looked up, and saw Bart standing in front of her, looking blurry. She was now sitting on the sand and couldn't remember actually sitting down...

"Hey, what's wrong?" he wanted to know.

"Not feeling well." She replied. "Couldn't be the drugs wearing off already, could it? It's hardly been three hours since my last fix..."

"Don't know," replied Bart, giving her a dose of clear heroine. "Got your shooting gear?"

'Clear dose for a change,' he thought. 'Should get her back in no time.'

She nodded.

"Perhaps I should go home and lie down a bit," she suggested.

"Okay." He agreed. "See you in another hour or two then?"

She nodded again, then walked away in the direction of her home.

More or less an hour later, she took the path back to the beach again, feeling slightly better. Bart waited for her on the pier.

"Feeling better?" he wanted to know.

She nodded.

"But something's wrong," she declared. "My heart is pounding faster than it ever did before, and there's a pressure on my chest. I'm also finding it hard to breathe..."

"That's normal after a spell like you've just had," he assured her.

But he knew he was lying... that it was because of the 'speedball' that he'd given her earlier, so soon after the speedball he'd given her that morning... and then a dose of heroine 3 hours before...

'I hope I didn't make a mistake, giving her yet another dose just now...' he thought...

"Perhaps," he said, "I should give you two fixes per day from now on."

Knowing that the mixture of coke and heroine will cause a deep depression and that the two drugs will actually increase the effect of both drugs, he began to worry.

"Will that be safe?" she wanted to know.

'A lot safer than what I gave you this morning!' he thought.

"Absolutely !" he replied. "You'll be okay in no time, then we can decrease it again, okay?"

She wasn't sure about that, but she nodded anyway.

Completely forgetting the dose of heroine he'd given her just two hours before, Bart also didn't take into consideration that she'd probably still be under the influence of the heroine that was in the second speedball...

They spent the rest of the day on the beach, Judy recruiting clients and Bart recruiting guinea pigs, making sure he got their cell numbers and, if possible, their residential addresses. That was, if they actually did have residential addresses.

When the sun began to set, Judy gave Bart the list of potential clients, together with their cell numbers.

Once that was done, Judy headed home, and Bart set out toward the research center...

*****

5 Pm

When Judy got home, she was feeling bad again. She was dizzy again, and almost blind. She could hardly see anything, and everything was swirling around her. Before she knew it, she passed out, falling on the floor...

Sunday, September 11th, 1988

And that's where Bart found her at **8 Am** the next morning... on the floor, hardly able to lift her head...

She attempted to get up when she saw Bart, but then passed out completely...

He felt her pulse. She was still alive.

He held a mirror in front of her nose. She was breathing, but barely...

"Hey Judda!" he tried to wake her up, to no avail...

'Shit!' he thought. 'Perhaps she's strong, mentally. But physically, she amounts to nothing... and that's partly my fault! I shouldn't have given her that many speedballs so soon after each other. Dammit! I cannot afford to lose her. Losing her would mean having to train someone else. There's just no time for that. Better get her to the Professor immediately...'

Bart picked her up and carried her to his car. 30 minutes later, he stopped at the ***MaitlonByTwo Research Center***...

Chapter 9 – Unexpected Revelation

Sunday, September 11th, 1988

8.30 am

Bart parked his silver 1958 Anglia in front of the main entrance of the research center. He dragged Judy out of the car, picked her up and carried her into the lobby.

Professor Melissa Maitlon looked up, and recognized Bart.

"Shit, Bart!" she exclaimed. "What the hell happened? Who is this girl?"

"She's the girl who's helping me recruit potential patients, Professor." He replied as he lay Judy down on the couch in a corner of the lobby. "I found her like this on her apartment floor this morning..."

The professor sharply drew in her breath as she recognized Judy.

"She's my daughter!" exclaimed the professor. "Did you know that?"

Suddenly, Bart went white in his face.

"No Professor," he replied. "I didn't know that. Had I known that, I would not have recruited her..."

She stared at Bart for about a minute, shook her head and picked up her cell phone. She dialled a number and waited.

" Rudolph," she then said. "Please come to reception.

*****

Wednesday, September 14th, 1988

10 am

Judy opened her eyes.

Slowly, but surely, she took in her surroundings.

'Wtf?' she thought. 'Where the hell am I? And how did I get here?'

She was lying in a bed with clean white linen, in a bedroom with white walls. There was one window, and on the bed table there was a glass with one red rose.

There was an IV in her arm, and she was connected to machinery that was monitoring her vital signs.

She sat up, looking for something to drink. She found a glass of water next to the glass with the rose. She took it and drank it, then waited for the familiar feeling of nausea that usually came after she ate or drank anything whatsoever...

The nausea didn't come.

She tried to stand, but realized that she was attached to a machine that kind of resembled a robot when she looked at it. She was attached to it by means of two tubes, each having a thick hypodermic needle attached to her arm. Blood ran freely through each tube.

'Wtf?' she thought. 'Why is my blood running through these tubes?'

"Good morning Judy!" said a female voice. "I suggest that you lie down again and don't try to stand at all."

Judy looked up and saw Shauna standing at the door.

"But why?" Judy wanted to know. "And what are you doing here?"

"First of all," replied Shauna, "I work here. And secondly, I'm here to take care of you while you recover from your overdose."

"Overdose?" inquired Judy.

"Yes," replied Shauna. "You've done too many 'speedballs' on one day."

"'Speedballs!'" exclaimed Judy.

"Yes, Girl." Replied Shauna. "Your pimp gave you two 'speedballs' on the same day, and then a dose of heroine. You very nearly didn't make it."

"What a piece of shit!" exclaimed Judy. "I'm gonna kill him!"

"If you ever see him again," replied Shauna, "I won't blame you if you actually do kill him. But that will just cause more problems for you. Rather just concentrate on the future, okay?"

Judy nodded.

"You're probably right," she agreed. "But tell me, why shouldn't I try to stand?"

"Well," replied Shauna. "You are attached to a dialyses machine. If you stood up and accidentally detached the tube that runs the blood back into your body, you could easily bleed out and die..."

"But is this procedure really necessary?" Judy wanted to know.

"Absolutely!" replied Shauna. "Without this procedure, you would've been dead already. That's how much of the drugs were in your blood. You were actually going blind already. Your father ordered that you be given dialyses for the next two days to make sure every little bit of it gets discarded..."

"My father?" inquired Judy. What does he have to do with this whole situation?

"In case you didn't realize this yet," replied Shauna, "you are not in a hospital. You are in your father's research center."

"I see," said Judy, frowning. "And what about my mother? She must be fretting and fuming right now..."

"That's kind of an understatement..." said Shauna.

"What if I want to go to the toilet?" Judy wanted to know.

"You won't need to," replied Shauna. "Your bladder is connected to a catheter. Your meals will be limited to IV liquids for now, so your gut excretions will be minimal, if any. For the next two days, you are stationary..."

"What if the catheter pulls out?" Judy wanted to know. "It must be quite a procedure in itself, getting it cleaned up..."

"Once again," replied Shauna, "you won't need to. I will be in here every now and then to check on you."

"How long have I been unconscious, by the way?" Judy wanted to know. "And how did I get here

"You've been unconscious for two days." Replied Shauna. And your pimp brought you in. He's been working for your father for the past two years, but didn't realize that you are the professor's daughter. Similarly, you father also didn't realize that you were being pimped by the person who'd been recruiting patients for him to experiment on. Your father was furious, and have fired your pimp. I suggest you accept it that way, and try to make sure that you don't upset your parents again. You are lucky that they didn't send you away when they realized that you began to use drugs again."

"So," Judy wanted to know, "Is it true that my parents are busy with something illegal?"

"Yes," replied Shauna. "But what they are doing is for the good of all mankind. When they complete this research, people will be able to reach their full potential much easier."

"How so?" Inquired Judy. "From what I understand, there is a man somewhere who chose to withdraw from society because my father botched up the experiment that was performed on him. What is the research center planning to do to relieve the pain that they have inflicted on that poor man? Also, why can people not just be left alone to decide for *themselves* whether they want to take a drug that will so-called 'increase their potential?'"

*****

Shauna completed Judy's routine examination, then left the room.

Judy was left alone with her thoughts.

'How could he?' thought Judy. 'And how could my mother? Even Shauna? Is there no morality left on the planet anymore? It's as though peoples' lives have become cheap! I'm disgusted! If I knew

how to disconnect from this stupid machine without dying, I would be out of here right now!'

Shauna was in and out during the day as she'd promised she would be.

'Is it because she cares,' thought Judy, 'or is it because she got instructions from my parents to check up on me and guard me so that I cannot escape?'

The next two days, Judy waited in anguish for when the machine would be disconnected. At last, at the end of the second day, Shauna removed the tubes, first the one running from her body and then, when all the blood had finally run back into her body, the other tube was removed.

Shauna then removed the catheter.

Judy was ecstatic to be free from machinery and other equipment...

"When can I go home?" Judy wanted to know after Shauna had removed the catheter.

"I don't know," replied Shauna. "Talk to your father. I'm sure he will have an answer for you..."

Judy pulled a sour face, but left it at that...

Chapter 10 – Escape

Friday, September 16th, 1988

6 am

Judy woke up with the absolute certainty in her mind that she would have to get out of the research center. She didn't trust her parents, and neither did she trust Shauna anymore. It was as though the devil himself had been released in the research center. The revelation of her parents having been at the very nucleus of what she'd been helping Bart with, sickened her to her very core...

'If I don't get out now, I won't be able to get out later,' she thought. 'I have to get to the police. They need to know everything that's going on here. But before I attempt to get out, I need to do some investigating myself'

Judy changed back into the clothes that she was wearing when she was dumped at the research center. Then she left her room, and walked down the passage.

She entered a room, and saw her father sitting at his desk. He was writing something on a sheet of paper.

"Hi Father," she said.

Without responding to her greeting, he beckoned her closer.

"Sit down, Judith," he said. "I want to talk to you..."

Without a word, Judy sat down, waiting.

Professor Maitlon completed what he was doing, then looked up.

"How did the latest detox go?" he wanted to know.

"Fine," she said, her voice dripping with sarcasm.

"Good." He replied. "So you'd say that it was a success?"

"Yes," she replied. "Why the dialyses, though?"

"It was necessary," he replied. "Besides the fact that it saved your life, it also rid your body of every molecule of the drugs..."

She nodded.

"So what is it exactly that you're doing here?" Judy wanted to know.

"We work with DNA, among others," he replied. "But you should know that, since you've closely worked with that pimp of yours…"

"He wasn't my pimp!" Judy retaliated. "More like a warden of sorts. He held me captive for more than two years, blackmailing me and coercing me into doing stuff that I didn't want to. I'm glad I'm rid of him…"

"That's good to hear," replied her father. "He's not your type."

She nodded.

"Yes, I know," she said. "I don't ever want to see him again. He almost killed me…!"

"When was the last time you've actually seen him?" the professor wanted to know.

"Obviously, before I blacked out in my apartment," she replied, kind of surprised that he'd asked her that question.

"I believe," she continued, "that he'd disappeared… That having come from Shauna…"

"Yes," replied her father. "That was after he ran away after I'd threatened to kill him."

"And would you?" asked Judy. "I mean, would you have killed him?"

"You bet!" he replied. "He got you addicted again, he coerced you into helping him recruiting people for illegal purposes and he coaxed you into leaving your home. Of course I would've killed him. And he'd better stay away from the research center, or I WILL kill him…"

"Why do you do what you're doing, Father?" Judy wanted to know. "Are people's lives not important to you?"

"It began as a hobby, Judith." He replied. "I used to experiment on altering the DNA structures of animals. My first success was to turn off the gene that was coded for the venom production of a snake. I've actually allowed the snake to bite me, and nothing happened to me."

"Later, he continued, when I've succeeded to alter the production rate of my pet rabbits, getting them to produce three times the number of babies than they used to, I figured I could perhaps help childless couples to have the children they deserved."

"And then," he further continued, "I began to alter the DNA of athletes, so that they could become invincible, each in their own sport. When a marathon runner died as a result of a failed procedure, I decided to cover it up. And from then on, the research center took off like a runaway robot. I cannot stop, since I dare not stop. The moment I do, we'll all be done for. Since we'll all be incarcerated..."

"I still think that you should stop!" she exclaimed. "Nothing bad needs to happen. Just close down the research center, sell your equipment and start over. Start on a clean sheet, so to speak..."

"I don't think that's possible," he replied. "I've taken this too far to just stop."

"How about trying?" she suggested. "Anything is possible if you put your mind to it. You yourself taught me that..."

"Okay, I'll try Judith," he said. "But for now, you'll have to excuse me. I have a procedure to prepare for..."

'I don't think he'll even try,' she thought. 'I think it's time to go. I also think it's time to sever this blood line and turn a page... begin fresh myself...'

"Okay, Father," she said. "I'll see you later then."

"Okay Judith." He said. "I'll talk to you later."

Judy turned around, but he called her back.

"Judith," he said. "Just one more thing before you go. I have a proposal for you."

"A proposal?" she inquired. "What kind of a proposal?"

"Well," he replied. Your mother and I have decided that you should move in. Come and live in the center, with us. As you should know, our house in Manhattan had been sold after you'd left, so we don't have a house anymore. How do you feel about coming to live here?"

"I don't know," she said, her heart sinking into her shoes. "Can I let you know tomorrow?"

"Tomorrow will be fine," he replied. "I'll see you here at 9 Am, tomorrow."

She gave him a thumbs up signal, then left his office.

*****

Judy couldn't stop thinking about her father's 'proposal.'

'He said that he has decided,' she thought. "But he didn't ask me, he merely told me. That doesn't sound like a proposal to me. It sounds more like an ultimatum. I don't think I should do it. But I will have to get out of here without them noticing, otherwise, I won't get out. They will stop my going the moment they see me leaving...'

*****

Saturday, September 17th, 1988

6 am

Early the next morning, Judy left her room. She wasn't quite sure where the main exit was, so she'd have to look for it.

Eventually, after about thirty minutes, she found it at the end of the passage that her room was in.

As she wanted to turn right towards the exit, she saw a movement

She looked in that direction and saw a young girl sneaking into a room but coming out again almost immediately, obviously looking for something.

'Perhaps she is also looking for the exit, trying to escape and needing help to find it,' thought Judy. 'I think I'll wait a while just in case. Perhaps I'll be able to help her...''

She went back to her room and entered it just in time to avoid being seen by Shauna, who was obviously looking for someone.

"Find her!" she heard her father say. "That procedure needs to be done right way!"

"Yes professor!" replied Shauna, then both Shauna and the professor went their separate ways...

Judy heard soft footsteps outside her door and opened it. It was the young girl. She reached out, grabbed the girl by the arm and pulled her inside the room, closing and locking the door behind her.

She put her finger over her lips to indicate that the girl should be silent.

"Hi!" whispered the girl. "I'm Grace. "Are you also a victim of this research center?"

"In a sense." Replied the girl. "I'm disgusted by what is going on here, but I don't believe my life is in danger. I am the professor's daughter, Judy. I was brought here by the person who used to supply my cocaine and heroine ... As a result of his stupidity, or negligence, or maybe just apathy, he gave me an overdose and I almost died. But perhaps it's a good thing it's happened, since now I know what my parents are up to, and what he... and they... are capable of."

"What, exactly, are they up to?" Grace wanted to know.

"Okay, here goes." Said Judy. "This was my bedroom for the last four days while they treated me to get the drugs out of my system. At least, that's one good thing that transpired from the whole negative incident.

"I've locked the door just so that nobody can enter unexpectedly…"

Grace nodded, looking apprehensive.

"So, Judy," inquired Grace. "Excuse me for not fully trusting you yet, but how do I know this is not a trick to capture me? I'm supposed to undergo a procedure at 11 am, but I don't wan to let them do it anymore…"

Judy shook her head.

"Don't allow any procedures to be done on you." She warned Grace. "Whatever it is, you will probably not survive it. I know, because I used to help that pimp of mine to recruit people for DNA experiments. There are two groups of people."

Judy went ahead, explaining the procedures that people were made to undergo at the center.

"One group kind of 'donates' DNA," continued Judy, "or a service of whichever kind, and the other group pays the research center to benefit from it. The research center offers the first group large amounts of money to participate in the 'program,' as they call it. They even go so far as to promise that the money will go to your family if something should happen to you during the tests or the experiments. Obviously, if you were one of the second group, you wouldn't have been here, running for your life."

"Yip!" replied Grace. "I'm definitely part of the first group. They've already extracted egg cells from me and had them fertilized by the sperm of a man whose wife cannot have babies. Also, they've altered the DNA of the embryos according to what the couple want the babies to look like and be able to do. Now they want to implant all eight of the embryos into my uterus at the same time! I'm not prepared to do that! What if all eight attaches to my uterus and grow to full term? What would I look like? My life would never be normal again!"

"Sounds like them." Confirmed Judy. "I've never had an idea of the evil that my parents are capable of..."

"Okay," said Grace. "I'm beginning to trust you. "How do I get out of here?

"Before I explain, listen carefully." Said Judy

Grace nodded.

"Fine." Said Judy. "When you continue in the direction you were going in when we met, walk to the end of the passage. Look to your right, and you will see the lobby. The door is always open, but be careful. Sometimes, either my mother, or Shauna, is at the reception desk. Careful that they don't see you..."

"How will I recognize your mother?" Grace wanted to know.

"You know Shauna," replied Judy. "If it's not Shauna, it will be my mother. They are the only females working here. Then once you've crossed the lobby, look to your left. There is a button on the wall that opens the main gate. Once you've pressed it, you'll have exactly thirty seconds to get though it before it will begin to close again. It takes another thirty seconds to close. In other words, you'll have a minute to get through the gate. The gate is about twenty yards from the lobby entrance. I hope you're a fast runner."

"Okay thank you , Judy." Said Grace. "I'd better be off, before they start looking in this direction as well. That Shauna character always comes to 'capture' me. She will definitely sound the alarm if she sees me..."

"Okay, Grace." Replied Judy. "Good luck, I hope you make it out in time..."

"Okay bye, Judy," said Grace. "Thank you for your help."

"Anytime!" replied Judy. When you get to the police, please tell them everything. This nonsense is not only illegal, it's also immoral and an abuse of human rights..."

"I promise." Said Grace.

Judy unlocked the bedroom door and inspected the passage to make sure it was safe. Then she gestured to Grace that she should go...

5 minutes later, Judy heard her father's bellowing voice shouting 'Close the gate!'

'I'd better go right way,' she thought, 'before they discover that I'm in on Grace's escape. I do hope she gets away...'

Judy left her room, walked to the lobby entrance and entered the lobby. Crossing the lobby, she saw her mother bending over the reception desk, absorbedly looking at something.

The exit door was open.

Looking at her mother, she began to walk to the exit.

'She's not looking at me,' thought Judy. Let's just hope it remains that way...'

Judy reached the exit without any incidents. She looked at the main gate, noticing that it was beginning to open.

"Go!" she heard her mother whisper. She looked at her mother, who signalled with her hand that she should go.

"Thank you," said Judy, then looked to the gate and ran for it.

"Close the gate!" she heard her father yell.

The gate began to close, but Judy made it just in time. She was out in the street just before the gate locked.

She looked around her, then walked in the direction of where she thought her apartment should be...

Chapter 11 – Justice for Judy

Saturday, September 17th, 1988

10 am

Judy walked, and walked, until she'd reached her apartment.

Inside, she prepared something to eat, then took a shower and got into a decent pair of jeans and a long T-shirt. She also put on a pair of sneakers.

Leaving her apartment, she began to walk to the police station. Upon reaching it, she entered the charge office.

Inside the charge office, she spoke to the officer on duty.

"I want to bring something to your attention, Officer." she said. "This is important, and it has to do with the people who have disappeared all around Los Angeles recently."

The officer wasted no time. He immediately made an internal call.

"Hi Chief," he said. "There's a girl here who says she's got info about the recent disappearances all across Los Angeles."

After a beat of silence, he spoke again...

"Okay right away, Chief!" He said. "I'm bringing her through..."

He hung up.

"The chief said he'll see you right away, Ma'am." He said. "Please follow me."

They walked down a short passage, and the officer knocked on a door on which the name 'Ron Quarry' was displayed.

"Come in!" Said a voice.

The officer opened the door and indicated to Judy that she should enter.

Judy entered, and waited for further instructions.

"Please sit down Ma'am," said Stitch.

"Thank you Sir." Said Judy as she sat down. "Please just call me Judy."

He held out his hand to greet her, and they shook hands.

'Firm grip.' He thought. 'she's making a good impression already...'

"I'm Stitch Quarry," he introduces himself.

"I'm Judy Maitlon," she returns the introduction.

"Okay, Judy,' began Stitch. "I understand that you have some information for us?" inquired Stitch.

"Yes, Sir," she replied. "I can tell you a lot of things about the recent disappearances, and the info will lead to the arrest of the perpetrators."

"And who are the perpetrators, Judy?" Stitch wanted to know. "Do you know these people personally?"

"Yes, Sir," she said softly, a tear running down her left cheek. "I know them all very well..."

"That's good news," said Stitch. "We've been trying to crack this case since the very first disappearance. So what can you tell us? And please... just call me Stitch."

"I don't quite know where to begin... uhm... Stitch," she replied. "By coming forward with this story, I'll be implicating not only myself, but my entire family, and also my former boyfriend, if you could call him that..."

"Wow..." he responded. "That sounds pretty hectic. How about starting at the beginning?" he suggested.

"The beginning would be at my parents' house in Manhattan, which they don't own anymore." Said Judy.

"Okay," said Stitch, pulling a writing pad closer to him. "You may begin..."

"My parents are both scientists, Stitch." began Judy. "And they own a research center, not too far from here."

"My life in my parents' house wasn't very happy." She continued. "In fact, it was extremely unhappy… They'd always put their work before me, and I was grossly neglected. I was just not priority to them…"

"That's a shame," said Stitch. "But continue…"

"I began to rebel against the manner in which my parents treated me," explained Judy. "But in essence, I was a very lonely child. And I built up a friend circle that could best be described as 'juvenile delinquents.'"

"Do you have any siblings?" Stitch wanted to know.

"No Stitch," replied Judy. "I am an only child. And perhaps, that's for the best…"

"And what do you have to do with the disappearances?" asked Stitch.

Judy sighed.

"This is going to be extremely difficult, Stitch." She replied. "But I have made a decision to go through with it, so here goes."

"Okay." He replied. "Continue please…"

Judy leaned forward, looking Stitch directly in the eyes.

"Stitch," she said. "I myself had quite a lot to do with the disappearances. Because of the way my parents treated me, I became a rebel. I wanted to show of in front of my peers, so I began to use drugs with them."

"What kind of drugs?" he wanted to know.

"At first," she replied, "It was Marijuana. I remained with Marijuana for quite a long time, but one night, one of my friends suggested we should try LSD. I would've done anything to spite my parents, so I agreed, just for the hell of it. I didn't really like the hallucinations that came with the LSD, so I stopped using it immediately before I've really started, directly after the first dose. I preferred to stay clear of it."

"And after that?" Stitch wanted to know.

"After that," she continued, "I've tried several other drugs, until, one night, I was dared by a group of my peers to try heroine."

"Heroine!" exclaimed Stitch. "That's quite hectic, and you don't strike me as someone who would go that far. What made you do it?"

"At first," she continued, "I hesitated. But you should know as well as I what peer pressure is like. Eventually, I caved in and I took my first dose of heroine. If, after that, I'd just left it at that, I would not have been hooked. But the new kind of euphoria that was the 'trademark' of heroine caught my attention. I was curious, so I took my second dose, and later my third, and then it became impossible to say 'no' to it, since it became unbearable to be without the drug…"

"Yes," Stitch continued, "I know all about what heroine does to teenagers. But could you please tell me now what your involvement was with the disappearances?"

"My personal involvement began after I kicked the habit the first time," she replied.

"And what made you decide to kick the habit?" Stitch wanted to know.

"I've overdosed," she replied, "so my parents got a nurse to stay with us for four weeks to help me get clean. Unfortunately, I didn't stay clean for too long. I've relapsed on the very first day after the nurse had left to take up her own responsibilities again."

"Why?" he inquired. "What exactly happened to make you relapse?"

"Listen, Stitch," she said. "I don't want to keep blaming my parents for everything, but it was the way my mother treated me when she spoke to me on the phone…"

Judy relayed the entire experience about Bart visiting her, leaving a dose of heroine on her doorstep and the effect her mother's words had on her.

"If she didn't say those words to me," said Judy, "I would not have relapsed."

"Such a pity." Replied Stitch.

"Yes, I agree." Said Judy. "If it wasn't for that relapse, I would never have gotten involved with the disappearances. And Bart knew exactly what he was doing when he coerced me to get involved with the disappearances... once he had me back on heroine, he'd used it to blackmail me into working with him to kidnap those people..."

"This... Bart." He said. "What car does he drive?"

"I may be wrong about the year model," she replied, "but I think it is 1958... an old silver Ford Anglia..."

"Well, I have news for you," said Stitch. "We have him in custody."

"Really?!" she exclaimed. "That really is news, Stitch! Good news, to be exact..."

"Would you mind participating in an identification session?" Stitch wanted to know. "He won't be able to see you at all..."

"No," she said. "I wouldn't mind at all. Just tell me when..."

"I will let you know." Said Stitch. "But first, let's complete your statement."

"Sure," replied Judy. "But just be warned, Stitch. What I'm about to tell you will shock you..."

"I think I'll be able to take it, Judy." Stich reassured her. "So let it fly..."

"Okay," she said. "But may I please have some water? My throat is dry from all the talking..."

"Sure, no problem." Replied Stitch, making an internal call, ordering two bottles of water.

Judy thanked Stitch for the water, then continued her story.

"As I said," she repeated, "This is going to be a shocker…"

"And as I've said," repeated Stitch, "I think I will be able to handle it, Judy."

"Fine," said Judy. "So without any further ado, let it be known that my parents, who own the *MaitlonByTwo Research Center*, are the main perpetrators in this two year old kidnapping saga."

"What!" Exclaimed Stitch. "Are we talking about that research center near the Hawthorne College Medical Center on Hawthorne Blvd?"

"Precisely that one!" confirmed Judy. "And to be exact, I've only learned about my parents' involvement three nights ago, when Bart just dumped me at the center after he nearly caused my death by giving me a drug overdose…"

Stitch whistled though his teeth.

"Well who would've guessed!" he exclaimed.

"Girl," he continued, "I think we've got a killer here!"

Judy told Stitch everything that she knew about the kidnapping saga, then left for home…

Sunday, September 18th, 1988

10 am

The next morning, Judy was sitting across from Stitch, after coming back to the police station.

Stitch dialled a number on his cell phone…

"Hi Bob," he said when the person at the other end answered.

"Yes, Chief!" said Bob. "How can I help?"

Bob had been driving around, looking for a girl that they'd lost a few nights before.

"Bob," said Stitch. "I want you to leave whatever you're busy with, and go to that research center on Hawthorne Blvd."

"What's cooking, Chief?" Bob wanted to know. "It's not like you to have me leave what I'm doing?"

"According to the declaration I got from someone very close to the owners of that research center, their goose is cooked." Replied Stitch. "I think we're gonna nail them, Bob."

"Allll...right!" Exclaimed Bob. "What do you want me to do, Chief?"

"Well," replied Stitch. "Not too much at the moment. Just go there, but stay at a safe distance. Without sight would be best. Record who goes in, and who comes out, okay?"

"Gotcha, Chief!" said Bob, and hung up.

*****

"So, Judy," said Stitch. "I would like to arrange for you to be a State Witness. Do you think you're up to that?"

Judy nodded.

"No problem, Stitch." She replied. "But before I give you my final consent, I would just like to know one thing. If I should do that, what exactly does that entail? The reason I'm asking, is the fact that you haven't said anything about my involvement in those disappearances. My parents are guilty of multiple kidnappings, mass murder and illegal experimenting on human subjects, without the consent of the subjects. They're manipulating people's DNA structures. Wouldn't my involvement make me an accomplice to all of that?"

"Well," said Stitch. "Technically, yes. But the judge will take into consideration the fact that you were a minor when that Bart character coerced you and blackmailed you into doing those things... also that you positively regret the fact of your involvement and that you have come to the police to spill the beans. And if you should turn to be a State Witness, the court may even grant you full immunity."

"Okay, Stitch," replied Judy. "Let's go for it..."

"Okay that's great, Judy." Said Stitch. "Could you wait outside my office for a few moments, I just need to discuss this with the official in charge of the State Witness Program."

"Sure," replied Judy as she stood up. She then left Stitch's office.

Five minutes later, Stitch opened the door and beckoned Judy inside.

"Okay, sit down, Judy." Said Stitch.

Judy sat down, facing Stitch.

"Good news, Judy," said Stitch, handing her a form to complete. "You are now officially admitted to the State Witness Program. Upon completion of the form I just gave you, we can work on further instructions."

*****

Judy handed her completed form to Stitch.

"So, Stitch," she wanted to know. "Where do I go from here?"

"Okay, Judy," replied Stitch. "Here's what I want you to do until further notice... Just lie low and keep your eyes and ears open. There could be people in there right now whose lives could be jeopardized, should your parents know that you've come to us to submit a statement."

"No problem, Stitch." Said Judy. One question, though: could I go back to the research center, enter it stealthily and keep a low profile. Do you think that could work?"

"No way!" exclaimed Stitch. "I couldn't allow you to do that!"

"Why not?" inquired Judy. "As you've just said, there could still be one or two so-called patients, waiting to be sent into oblivion. As it is, I think I've heard what I thought was a little girl crying last night. What if there really is a little girl, and I could've prevented her death, but I didn't because I wasn't there to help her?"

"Judy," replied Stitch. "It really is not a good idea. I want you to stay put, is that clear?"

"Yes," replied Judy, "but what if there is a little girl needing help?"

"Okay, Judy," replied Stitch. "You've heard me speak to my officer Bob. He will be watching the place until I tell him otherwise. So it's really not necessary for you to risk your life..."

Judy nodded.

"Okay, I agree with you, Stitch," she said. "What else can I do to help?"

"Well," replied Stitch, "come to think of it, we're planning an ID session for that Bart character today. Would you like to participate?"

"No problem," replied Judy.

"Great!" said Stitch. "Please be here at 1 Pm. Also, just to warn you. There will be someone else to participate whom you might be familiar with. I cannot disclose who the person is, right now, but the two of you will meet up before the session, after which you will be called into the room one by one..."

"Okay, Stitch," said Judy. "I will see you at 1 Pm then..."

Judy got up and left the office. She took a seat inside the charge office, but the attending officer redirected her to an interrogation room just for the time being...

*****

Monday, September 19th, 1988

10 am

"Hi Bob, this is Stitch. Talk to me..."

Stitch put the document down that he'd been reading before the phone rang.

Judy also sat at the desk, facing Stitch.

"Hi Chief," said a voice. "This is Bob. Just thought you would want to know. I have just picked up that little girl that we've been so frantically looking for most of the past two days!"

"Oh my gosh! Bob!" exclaimed Stitch. "Well done! Where did you find her? And when?"

"Well, Chief," continued Bob. "I would've loved to take all the credit for this one, but I can't! You were right about that research center. The little girl came running out of their yard and then just walked up to me and asked for my help..."

"Did you see anyone else come out of there?" Stitch wanted to know.

"I did not specifically notice anyone," replied Bob.

"Okay, no problem," said Stitch. We'll catch them all eventually..."

"So what was the little girl's story?" Continued Stitch.

"She told me a fantastic tale about how she'd escaped from that research center," replied Bob. "According to her, she was in some kind of a room where her science teacher was in the process of altering her DNA. Apparently, she got some power from her subconscious mind, which helped her escape. And then she found me..."

"Her science teacher?" inquired Stitch. "Can you just hang on a second, Bob? I want to ask someone something..."

"Okay, no problem, Chief," replied Bob. "I'm hanging..."

"Judy," inquired Stich. "Does your father perhaps teach science classes somewhere?"

"No," replied Judy. "My mother does, but only on a part time basis. She teaches science to the Grade 6 students at the Grandview Elementary School on 24th Street, Manhattan Beach."

"Your mother?" said Stitch. "Is she also a scientist working at the research center?"

"Yes," replied Judy. "But she's not as involved as my father."

"Okay thank you, Judy," said Stitch. "You've been very helpful."

"Hi Bob," said Stitch into the receiver of the phone. "You still there?"

"Yes, Chief," said Bob. "Still hanging."

"You still got the little girl with you?" Stitch wanted to know.

"Yes," replied Bob. "She's not with me in the car right now, I had to bring her to her home to get dressed. She was only dressed in a surgical pinafore and a pair of paper slippers. I'm waiting for her to come back to the car. I've told her to put the surgical attire in a paper bag and bring it with, since we may need it as evidence…"

"Okay, great." Said Stitch. "Just make sure she does get back to you. I don't trust those lot at the research center…"

"I agree, Chief!" replied Bob. "I don't trust them either. If she doesn't appear within the next few seconds, I'll go into the house and find her…"

"That will be great, Bob," said Stitch. "You just make sure she comes to the station with you… and make sure she's alive when you do that…"

"Will do, Chief." Said Bob. Okay here she is now… and she's alive. I'll see you just now at the station…"

"Okay see you just now then, Bob." Said Stitch and hung up.

*****

"Seems you were right about the little girl, Judy." Said Stich. "Apparently, she'd escaped and ran right to where my officer, Bob, was hiding while watching the research center. Just as well I'd instructed him to do that…"

"Oh, thank goodness!" exclaimed Judy. "I knew I didn't imagine that. Also there was another woman who'd escaped using my directions. She'd escaped an hour or so before I left…"

"Do you know the name of the woman?" Stitch wanted to know.

"Yes," replied Judy. "She said her name was Grace. Apparently, my parents wanted her to be a surrogate mother for a childless couple. According to my parents, the woman is infertile. My father had altered the DNA structure of the in vitro embryos, and he wanted to implant eight embryos into Grace's uterus. Grace didn't feel up to carrying eight babies to full term, so she pulled out of the deal..."

"Wow!" Exclaimed Stitch. "This is getting weirder and more wonderful by the minute! Good for her that she'd pulled out, though.

"Yes," said Judy. "I agree with you. Her pulling out almost cost her her life, though! I just hope there aren't any more people there waiting to receive 'procedures,' as my father calls them."

"Yes," replied Stitch. "I agree with you. As soon as bob drops off the little girl, he should go back to see if anyone else comes out..."

"Stitch," said Judy. "If you need to know for sure whether those people who'd disappeared are still alive, then perhaps you should get a search warrant and search the research center. I know for a fact that they have a whole room full of corpses. I know that since I've seen it. I've been in the room..."

"Thank you, Judy," said Stitch. "And I think we'd better do that real quick, to keep them from getting rid of all those corpses. "How many are there? Do you know?"

"At least ten." Replied Judy. "That is what I've seen with my own eyes. There could be more, though."

"Okay, I'll make work of getting the warrant." Said Stitch. "Meanwhile, let me take you to the room where the Identification of Bart will take place..."

"Okay," she agreed, getting up from the chair.

They walked to the room, and Stitch briefed Judy as to the procedure.

"Whatever you do," said Stitch. "Don't worry. He will not be able to see- or hear you…"

"Thank for telling me that, Stitch." Said Judy. "I was quite worried that he might see me. I don't want him to see me, and after today, I don't want to ever see him again…"

"I don't blame you." Said Stitch.

They entered a darkened room. There was a window connecting the darkened room to another much smaller room. A bright light was shining in the smaller room.

He showed her exactly where to sit.

Six men walked into the smaller room on the other side of the mirror. Each man was carrying a number. They held a number. They were numbered from 1 to 6. Bart's number was 5.

"Don't worry," said Stitch. "As I told you before… he won't be able to see- or hear you at all. The other side of the window is a mirror…"

Relieved, she nodded.

"Okay Judy," said Stitch. "I'm gonna leave you now to get that search warrant. Good luck!"

She nodded and then he left.

"Okay Ma'am," asked the attending officer. "Do you recognize the man who had blackmailed you and had given you drugs on a regular basis?"

Judy didn't need much time. She would recognize Bart anywhere.

"No 5!" she said. "It is No 5. He's the one!"

"Thank you Ma'am." Said the officer. "That will be all for now."

The men was led out of the smaller room, and then the light was switched off.

"I'd say that was a positive identification," said the officer…

Short Interlude

They say that hell is the ultimate furnace.

I tend to disagree...

What bigger 'hell' could there be than eternity without God? I think that that is precisely what hell is... eternity without the One who is the ultimate *Source of everything*... the One who has given you life... the One who, thus far, during your entire life, has provided everything that you could ever need...

There is another kind of 'hell...' an extension (or attachment) to the 'hell' that's called 'eternity without God,' and therefore in essence a part of that void eternity... this 'hell' is being forced to indulge in ones favorite 'indulgence' for eternity... to never be able to shed that which has caused the 'hell' in the first place...

Take alcohol, for instance. Or any other drug, for that matter. Being a slave to the drug would be 'hell' in itself. But to be unable to stop abusing the monster of drugs, which like a dragon, keeps relighting the furnace, perpetually increasing the heat of addiction? To forever be unable to shed what has caused you to not be able to connect with the only *Source of Life in Abundance* and subsequently not being able to be free from that 'hell?' Could there ever be a more prominent and ever present 'hell...?'

Whether nicotine, or alcohol, or heroine, or cocaine, or PCP, or prescription drugs, or even just Cannabis... being addicted is the ultimate furnace... the ultimate 'hell.' Without God to help you overcome it, your journey away from addiction would be so much harder... that is *if* you even succeed...

In the case of this story, the addicted person did, in fact, become clean of drugs, and, subsequently, the heat of the furnace had dissipated...

Section II – Burinda

Chapter 12 – Stalker

Burinda was a happy elementary school girl who had lots of friends. Perhaps the fact that she had caring and loving parents had everything to do with the fact that, at the beginning of one summer vacation when she'd encountered a dangerous situation that could've been life threatening, she took it on full stride, worked through it like her dad had taught her and landed on her feet without even being phased by it when it was eventually over...

*****

Tuesday, September 12th, 1988

6 pm

12-year-old Burinda Davison was a Grade 6 learner at the Grandview Elementary School on 24th Street, Manhattan Beach, Los Angeles, California.

School was out for the Summer Vacation, and Burinda decided to join a few of her friends for a long, relaxing walk on Manhattan Beach.

"See you later, Mom!" she announced her departure to the beach.

"Okay, Honey." Replied her mom. "But be careful out there. Keep your eyes and your ears open. I don't want you to become part of statistics. The most recent case was just yesterday, when that couple from Florida disappeared from the beach pier..."

"I'll be careful, Mom," Burinda reassured her mom. "Don't worry, I'll be with my school friends the whole time."

"Good!" said Mrs. Davison. "It's always safer to be among friends."

She waved, and Burinda waved back.

"And stay away from the pier!" Said her mom. "Most of the disappearances seem to happen there…"

"Will do!" replied Burinda as she took off on a trot, well knowing that the pier was precisely where she was going to meet her friends…

*****

6 pm

Burinda had thoroughly enjoyed her time on the beach with her friends, where they'd been killing some time after school.

Burinda was alone now, since her friends had to turn off into the streets where they were living. It was only about 100 yards from her home when the last of her friends, Henry, turned toward his home. He wanted to walk her home, but she said she'd be okay.

It was already almost dark, though, and Burinda was afraid. Thoughts of the recent disappearances of people living in all across Los Angeles, but especially in Manhattan, came to her mind.

Most of the people who went missing had disappeared after dusk from the streets of the Central Business district, but there were a few who'd disappeared from the beach, specifically around the Manhattan Beach Pier… and mostly from underneath the pier, where the waves were breaking against the pillars supporting the pier.

Just the day before, a young couple from Florida were on top of the pier admiring the moonlight. They were warned about the disappearances, and promised not to stay very long. They just wanted to enjoy some sightseeing. They were never seen again, and were reported missing by their parents the next day.

'I shouldn't have stayed on the beach that long,' she thought. 'Mom warned me about all those cases of people disappearing lately. What was I thinking?'

Almost home, she thought she'd heard something, and looked back.

'Someone is out there!' she thought. 'Behind that rock! Better run for it! Before I become a victim too...!'

Burinda carefully turned her head in the direction of the rock and saw the dark outline of a man's head sticking out above the rock. Judging by the height at which the head was silhouetted, this man had to be a giant...

Burinda couldn't make out any of the man's features in the growing darkness of the increasing afternoon twilight.

The rest of the man was hidden behind the rock. Only his head was fully visible as he peeked over the rock, staring at Burinda...

Burinda was only about ten yards from home. She took off, running the last few yards.

'Is he following me?' she wondered...

But she couldn't dare looking back or over her shoulder, for fear of falling and then becoming a victim of whomever (whatever?) it was that was taking the disappearing people.

When she reached her front gate, she stopped briefly and looked back.

'Oh no!' she said to herself. 'He's now standing next to the rock, staring at me! And he's huge!'

She walked into her yard and quickly closed the gate. The urge to run into her home took her, but she didn't run, for fear of startling her parents.

She slowly walked into her home, then began to cry.

"Burinda?" said her father. "What's wrong Honey? Are you all right?"

Burinda told her father what had happened. He ran outside to see if he can see the stalker, but the thug had already disappeared.

*****

Wednesday, September 13th, 1988

6 pm

The next night, the same thing happened. This time, Burinda was on her way home from one of her friends. They were spending some time together to make some plans for the summer vacation.

She stole a glance to where she saw the giant man the previous night, but there was nothing. The rock stood alone.

'But I can feel him!' she thought, 'He's definitely here somewhere!'

She kept walking, looking back every minute or so. Try as she might, she couldn't see the man. But she knew that he was hiding there somewhere. She could feel his essence, so to speak...

Suddenly, she could hear fast footsteps, like someone running. She also took off running.

Feeling a compelling urge to look back, she couldn't help it. She just had to look back!

Burinda turned around, just in time to see someone duck behind the trunk of a large tree!

'Could I have imagined that?' she thought to herself. Oh no! Better get home fast... don't want to fall prey to some pervert...'

Burinda stopped running, but walked very fast. She heard the footsteps again and walked even faster.

She then slowed down to glance over her shoulder. Listening intently, she realized that she'd stopped hearing the footsteps.

She kept looking back, still feeling like someone was watching her. The whole time of her short path from her friend's home, she kept getting this feeling... and she kept seeing shadows ducking behind trees, rocks and shrubs.

Burinda felt tempted to run, but decided against it.

'Running again would only attract more attention.' She thought...

At some stage, when she was in the process of looking back to see if it could be that same giant man following her, Burinda tripped over something and lost her balance. She yelped as she got a fright, and grabbed onto a tree to steady herself.

The cat over which she tripped made a hissing noise.

Burinda looked down and saw the cat.

"Stupid cat!" she yelled at it.

The cat hissed at her again, then fled into the darkness...

Burinda continued walking.

'I wonder why people can't keep their stupid cats in their homes,' she said to herself. 'Cats will leave their owners in a flash when they feel like it, yet they are allowed to do exactly what they please; but when dogs accidentally get out of their yards, everybody is up in arms! Yet dogs will remain faithful to their human companions under any circumstance, no mater what.'

Burinda reached the gate to her yard and looked toward her front door. She stopped in mid-stride.

'What the hell?' thought Burinda. 'A dark shadow had just vanished behind that shrub next to the door. So now the stalker is here as well? That looked more uncanny than I'm comfortable with. Wonder if it's safe to approach..."

"Hello Burinda." Said her father. "Are you all right, Sweetie?"

Burinda heaved a sigh of relief.

'Thank goodness, it's my dad...' she thought.

Burinda ran into her dad's arms, crying.

"Oh Daddy!" She sobbed. "That stalker followed me again, this time from my friend's home. And I think that might have been him, behind that shrub over there. It's a bit dark already, but I think it's the red Hibiscus. I could've sworn I just saw him duck behind it... that's why I hesitated after coming through the gate, when I looked toward the door and saw the movement of someone ducking into the shrub right next to the door..."

"Come walk with me, Honey," said her father. "I will check the shrub and everything surrounding it. And I swear! I will kill anyone trying to hurt you...!

"Thank you Daddy," she replied. "I'm so relieved that you are here. The thought of being alone and having to walk through the garden toward the door petrified me..."

"Calm down now, Sweetie," replied her father. "I'm here, and you are safe."

The two of them walked to the front door.

"I'm really terrified of this night stalker, Daddy." Said Burinda. "He's a giant... and there's a specific vibe... it's as though I can 'feel' him, even though I cannot see him...

"I don't blame you, Baby" replied her father. "It's just natural that you'd be afraid..."

"But this is different, Daddy," she tried to explain. "It's almost... supernatural. Not sure how to describe it..."

As they reached the shrub where Burinda saw the shadow, her father took a good look in and around the shrub, but he found nothing.

"Okay," he said. "It seems to be all clear Pumpkin. Cannot see anybody here."

"Thank you so much, Daddy." She replied. "I just wish this would end now. Ever since people began to disappear all around Manhattan, I sometimes get startled even by my own shadow. Tonight was particularly bad. I heard running footsteps behind me three times in a row. And I saw shadows disappearing behind shrubs. And now this experience of seeing someone in my own yard..."

"Yes, that sounds hectic." He said. "I think, just until this bout of disappearances blow over, I should pick you up from wherever you're at, whenever you need a ride home..."

"That will be such a relief, Daddy," replied Burinda. "I'm a nervous wreck right now. I feel safer already."

"Anytime, my baby." He said, hugging her. "You're precious to me and your mom. Come, let's go inside. We need to get out of the dark. I think we will both feel better inside, where the lights are turned on..."

Chapter 13 – Captured

Wenesday, September 14th, 1988

5 pm

The next afternoon, Burinda was waiting for her Dad to pick her up. She had arranged with him to get her in front of the School of Dance & Music on Aviation Blvd after her ballet lesson.

Fearfully, she consulted her cell phone for what seemed to be the 1000th time. Realizing that it is after 5.30 pm already, she once again dialed her father's cell number.

"Hi, this is Richard Davison…," announced the voicemail salutation for what felt to Burinda like the millionth time. She sighed, waited until the beep, then spoke:

"Daddy, where *are* you?" she said to the recording. "The sun is setting and it will get dark soon! I don't want to still be here when it's dark. I can already feel the presence of that stalker. It's uncanny…"

Burinda heard something. She looked up and thought she saw someone duck behind a shrub on the sidewalk across from where she was sitting on the step in front of the closed and locked School of Dance & Music entrance gate.

Squinting against the rays of the setting sun, trying to see who it was, she couldn't make out much. Fact is, the shrub was right between her and the sun, making it difficult to see. All she could see was the dark silhouetted outline of the shrub, so she couldn't make out whether it was actually a human that she saw.

Diagonally across from her, she saw an old silver Anglia parked in the street. A man was sitting behind the wheel.

'I could swear that man is looking right at me.' she thought.

Anxiety and immanent tears unmistakably evident in her 12-year-old-girly-voice, she now yelled into the handset.

"Daddy!"

Then she calmed down.

"Daddy!" She said, "I think someone's watching me! I know you told me to wait for you, no matter what, but you also taught me that from a very young age that determination can be my best friend when or if I get into a situation where I am in any kind of danger , and that I shouldn't let fear or anything else overcome me. I am in danger now and I am determined not to let it overcome me. I'm gonna walk home. So don't come pick me up okay? I'll see you at home…"

Burinda disconnected the call and put the phone in her sweater pocket. She put the straps of her backpack onto her shoulders, fastened it around her waist and began to run.

Looking over her shoulder, she again tried to spot the person she thought was behind the shrub. However, the sun still made it difficult for her to see anything in that direction…

She turned to look back in the direction she was running, and shrieked when she unexpectedly bumped into someone and lost her balance. She caught sight of a hairy hand shooting out towards her and grabbing her shoulder, steadying her and keeping her from falling…

"Here now, young lady," said a man's deep voice, "where are you going so fast?"

Still looking downward due to almost falling, Burinda saw a large pair of boots. She slowly looked up… and up… and up until her eyes reached the face of the man. He was huge! Easily over 7 feet tall…

'The giant!' She thought. 'It must be him!'

Burinda screamed, turned around and ran back to where she came from.

She heard footsteps following her… the same footsteps she'd heard the previous two nights.

"Oh Daddy, where are you?" she sobbed.

Suddenly, she heard someone yell!

"Halt!" yelled the person. "What do you think you're doing?!"

The footsteps stopped.

"Mind your own business, you piece of crap!" yelled the giant. "I've had enough of your shit, already...!"

And then Burinda heard the giant take off in the direction she wanted to go... to where her home was...

She turned around, staring at the disappearing body of the giant...

'Oh no!' she thought. 'Now I won't be sure whether it's safe to enter my home! And what if he decides to go in and harm Mom and then wait for me?'

She just stood there, staring, until the man who was sitting in the old silver Anglia approached her.

She prepared to take off again, but the man reached her just in time to catch her and hold onto her shoulder, forcing her to remain standing.

"What are you doing here all alone in this neighborhood?" the man wanted to know. "Don't you know it will be dark soon? And that it could be dangerous for little girls like you to walk alone outside after dark?"

"Yes, I do," replied Burinda, tears now running freely over her cheeks, her bright blue eyes shining brightly in the last lingering morsel of sunlight. A ray of sun got caught in her copper colored hair, forming a golden halo around her head.

'What a beautiful little girl,' thought the man. "Wonder how long that's gonna last, though...'

"If you know that," he said aloud," "what are you doing out here? And where are you going?"

The man kept staring at her, indicating by means of facial expression that he was waiting for a reply...

Burinda began to cry.

"There there, little girl," said the man, pacifying her. "I am here to help. Just tell me where you are going…"

Still sobbing, Burinda begins to explain.

"I was waiting for my dad to pick me up after my ballet lesson, and he didn't pitch. I'm still waiting for him. He's also not answering his cell phone. It's going on voicemail all the time. He would never just leave me waiting. It's just not like him, so I'm worried. I was walking home, but now I can't anymore because that big man ran off in the direction of my home. I think I should just walk and look for my dad instead. I need to find him in case that giant man goes into our home and hurts my mom"

"She'll be fine, you'll see," said the man, smiling, sounding almost sympathetic. "And so will your dad. Perhaps I can help you out. You don't live very far from here, do you?"

"No not really. About 2 miles," replied Burinda hopefully, anticipating him offering her a ride. She just couldn't stay in front of the Dance School any longer, in case the giant man came back.

"Where do you live?" asked the man.

She told him her address.

"Okay, tell you what…" he offered, "I just need to pick up my little girl form horse riding lessons, and then I will give you a ride home, okay?"

Openly relieved, she nodded 'yes.'

"Thank you Sir," she said.

"You're welcome, young lady," he replied, his eyes gleaming with anticipation as he thought of the reward he would be getting for bringing yet another young one to the research centre. He put his arm around her shoulders and led her to the Anglia. Not far from where the Anglia was parked, was a parked black Ford sedan.

As the man opened the passenger door for her to get in, he inconspicuously threw the kiddy lock so that it couldn't be opened from the inside.

Bart Cash couldn't believe his luck. He'd been watching Burinda for days, considering how to go about enticing her to get into his car… and here she was… literally bounding into it all by herself.

'The professor will be so pleased with me for this pound of flesh,' he thought.

As Cash closed the passenger door, essentially trapping Burinda inside the car, the driver of the black Ford started the engine… and as Cash pulled away to go and commit dark deeds, the black car silently slipped onto the road behind him…

Chapter 14 – Rescued

Wenesday, September 14th, 1988

5.30pm

The song *The Sound of Silence by Paul Simon,* began to play on the radio.

"My ultimate favorite," said Ron (Stitch) Quarry to nobody in particular, turning up the volume.

Stitch began to sing along, enjoying himself. He relaxed as the lyrics resonated with his inner self. Stitch is not a bad singer himself, and any potential passenger would have enjoyed listening to him.

Stitch was driving through Downtown Manhattan. He was looking for anything that could've been a clue to where the missing citizens of Los Angeles, specifically citizens of Manhattan, could've been disappearing to, and what their fate and condition might've been… but to no avail.

He wasn't driving very fast, since he didn't want to miss anything that might have been important. He had the air conditioner on, since it was a hot Los Angeles day in spite of a light shower of rain. The windows were turned up and the brand new Merc's tires were taking it casually, as if reluctant to take it a bit faster.

Stitch had just been promoted to Chief Commanding Officer at the LAPD and the Merc was part of the perks.

Stitch is not used to slow speeds, but the soothing effect of *Paul Simon's* masterpiece made Stitch feel drowsy. He had a dreamy expression on his face. Having just left the hospital, he couldn't be happier. His wife, Amy, had given birth to their first child about an hour before… a baby son of almost nine pounds.

He smiled as he thought back to that magic moment when little Ronnie cried out his little lungs for the very first time…

Stitch had just come back from an important meeting when he was informed that the ambulance had taken Amy to the hospital.

Cream colored suit, black shirt, and a light grey tie with black pinstripes on it. That was his attire when he ran into the hospital, through the corridors and into the delivery room.

And presently, he was roaming the streets of Manhattan in search of a clue... anything that could lead him to the missing people... so far, 37 people had disappeared without a trace...

The sound of *Paul Simon's* voice stopped suddenly... abruptly... as his phone rang. He took a long breath to recover from his singing.

The phone was on 'hands free,' so he clicked the 'accept call' button on the steering wheel.

"Hi, this is Stitch." He said. "Talk to me..."

"Hi Chief," said a voice. "This is Bob. Just thought you should know. That suspicious Bart character has picked up an elementary school girl and is on his way somewhere. Looks like he's about to leave Manhattan. Do you want me to keep following him?"

"Absolutely!" replied Stitch. "Keep following him until you know where he's going, then let the police in that area know. And lie low. I don't want him to spot you following him..."

"You got it, Chief!" said Bob.

Bob Binkley had recently been promoted to Detective I. Stitch had chosen him to investigate the Los Angeles disappearances.

"Okay great!" replied Stitch. "And anything suspicious, you let me know okay?"

"Okay Chief." Said Bob. "I'll call you the moment I see anything strange..."

"Great!" replied Stitch. "Will talk to you later, then..."

Stitch hung up...

He resumed driving through the streets of Downtown, Manhattan.

The song *The Sound of Silence by Paul Simon* continues to play and Stitch resumes his singing.

Stitch was just beginning to relax again, when The sound of *Paul Simon's* voice abruptly stopped... he repeated the ritual of taking a long breath to recover from his singing while the phone frantically tried to get his attention.

He clicked the 'accept call' button on the steering wheel again, pulling a face.

'I'm not ready for this again...' thought Stitch. 'I hope he has some real info for me this time...'

"Hi, this is Stitch." He said. "Do you have some real info for me this time?"

"Indeed Chief!" replied Bob. "He's stopped and parked the car. Looks like he's booked into a motel."

"You're telling me he's already booked a room?" Stitch wanted to know. "Where? Which Motel? Has he checked in already?!" Stitch exclaimed.

"Uhhhm... nope! Looks like he's doing that now."

"Damn! And where's the girl?"

"He's left her in the car."

"What!?" Exclaimed Stitch. "Is the freak crazy?"

"Must be." Replied Bob. "No sane person would leave an innocent young girl in a car while he himself books into a cozy motel..."

"O...kay." Says Stitch. "Which motel?"

"The Travelodge in Telegraph Rd," replied Bob.

Stitch whistles through his teeth...

"Cozy indeed!" he exclaimed. "Seems our target has some cash to throw around...!"

"Yip!" agreed Bob.

"And where are *you*?" Stitch wanted to know

"Sitting in my trustworthy old black Ford across the road from the Travelodge. What do you want me to do?"

"Dammit man!" Exclaimed Stitch. "The girl's life is at stake!! What do you *think* I want you to do!? You need to get her out of that car and at a safe place as in YESTERDAY!"

"No problem Chief!" said Bob, getting out of hid Ford. "I'm running towards the car as we speak..."

""Good!" said Stitch. " Just hurry! I'm turning the Merc around. On my way there now, but you don't get her out of that car right now, she could be dead by the time I get there! These are not just ordinary criminals. They're a lethal syndicate. I'm bringing the squad with me. And please let me know if anything, negative or positive, happens, okay? Oh! And text me his room number so that the squad can get to work immediately. We cannot allow the freak to get away again...!"

"Will do Chief!" replied Bob and hung up?

"Sometimes, you can be so sluggish," said Stitch to nobody in particular, since Bob couldn't hear him anymore.

He hung up.

The radio began to blare again. It startled Stitch, since *The Sound of Silence* had apparently completed its appearance on the air and was replaced by some hard rock song that Stitch didn't recognise. His first inclination was to fling the phone out the window, charging the damage against 'collateral damage,' but he didn't think that would work...

'I hope he hurries up!' thought Stitch.' If he botches this up, I'll personally have his ass in a coffer sooner than he can say 'Jack Robinson.' I hope he realises that...'

Stitch turned off the radio, leaving only the 'real' sound of silence.

'Better get going,' he thought, 'Travelodge is still quite a distance from here...'

*****

6 pm

Bob reached the car and shattered the window in order to get Burinda out of the battered 1958 Ford Anglia. He reached through the broken window into the car, unlocked the door and tried to open the door from the inside, but couldn't.

"Oh!" he said to nobody in particular. "Kiddie lock...!

He withdrew his hand and opened the door using the outside door handle.

A quick glance told him that the girl was unconscious, lying on the back seat. He quickly listened for breathing and felt for pulse.

'She's alive...' he thought. 'Better get her out of here quick...!'

He picked her up and drew her out of the car.

'Alive, yes,' he thought, 'but dead weight. Better get on with it...'

Bob's black Ford was parked diagonally across the road, and out of sight from where the Anglia was parked. He carried Burinda to his car, letting her lie down on the back seat. He set the kiddy locks on both back doors.

'She's probably in shock,' he thought. 'One never knows what she might do when she wakes up.'

He got in behind the wheel, started the car and slowly drove away, dialing Stitch's number.

*****

6.15 pm

The sound of the phone startled Stitch again, but he didn't show an interest again to toss the phone out the window.

"Hi, this is Stitch." He said. "Do you have some good news for me this time?"

"Hi Chief!" replies Bob. "Yes indeed. I got the girl out of the car, driving away from the motel as I speak..."

Stitch heaved a sigh of relieve.

"Well done!" he said. "Put as much distance as you can between yourself and that motel, then take her to the station."

"Negative, Chief!" replied Bob. "I will need to get her to a hospital right away. She's been drugged. Her pupils are dilated and her vital signs are almost non-existent..."

"Shit!" exclaimed Stitch. "Do that then, and as quickly as you can..."

"Roger that, Chief!" said Bob, I'll take her to the 'Whittier Hospital,' which is about 7 miles from here...

Bob set course for the Whittier Hospital in Washington Blvd...

Chapter 15 –Vanished

Wenesday, September 14th, 1988

7 pm

After clearing his head, Stitch was feeling a new rush of adrenaline coursing through his veins.

He contacted the station, instructing them to send out three squad cars to the Travelodge Motel in Telegraph Road.

Weaving between the cars on the road, he gripped the wheel tighter and stepped down hard on the gas. The clock was ticking; the stakes were genuine, and the consequences could be disastrous.

Stitch speeded up as he put the Merc's full potential to the test.

"Come on, Bob!" he said to nobody in particular. "I need that room number…!"

As if in reply, his phone buzzed. The address and room number showed up on his phone as a text.

'Thank God he didn't forget!' thought Stitch. 'We cannot afford to let this freak get away!...'

He drove as fast as he could take the Merc, given the traffic.

Then he saw the name of the motel flashing out an invitation: 'Travelodge…'

He saw the exit ahead of him and took it.

He began to look for an inconspicuous place to park, which was also out of the range of any cameras. He decided on a residential street behind the motel.

Stitch stopped at the back of the Travelodge Motel. Not too long after that, Bob stopped next to him.

Both got out, greeting each other.

"Is the girl okay?" Stitch wanted to know.

"Not sure," replied Bob, looking concerned. " I hope so. They are trying to stabilize her. Looks like the jerk had given her a 'speedball' or something similar. They cannot determine the exact ratio heroine to cocaine, since it was injected into a vein. They found the mark where the needle went in…"

"Damn!" exclaimed Stitch. "No wonder she hardly has any life left in her… hope she makes it, poor girl…"

Three squad cars arrive one after the other.

"Hey, Guys!" said Stitch. "Please, no sirens and no lights. We need to catch the freak unawares…"

"Roger that, Chief!" replied all three officers in unison.

Stitch pulled a cap down over his face and grabbed his baton. He gestured to Bob to follow him and instructed the other three officers to stay put and stay alert.

It took the two of them about three minutes to find Room Number 2 and to start banging on the door.

"Police!" Shouted Stitch. "Open this door!"

No response…

"Police!" repeated Stitch. "I said open this door!"

Still no response…

Stitch decided to kick in the door. It gave way after the third attempt.

"Stay here," said Stitch to Bob.

Bob nodded, giving Stitch the 'thumbs up' sign.

Stitch cautiously moved into the room, looking around.

Cash was lying on the bed, half naked. A half naked girl was lying on the bed next to him.

Stitch indicated to Bob to enter the room. Bob entered.

"Handcuff them," instructed Stitch.

Bob took out his handcuffs and handcuffed Cash. Then he took another pair of handcuffs offered by Stitch, and handcuffed the woman.

They kept sleeping during the entire procedure. Try as they might, the officers couldn't wake the pair of criminals...

"They must be under the influence of something," said Stitch, watching the criminals for movement.

"Only one solution here..." said Bob.

Stitch followed the trajectory of Bob's field of vision and nodded.

"Go ahead," said Stitch.

Bob walked over to the coffee table and grabbed a large pitcher of water standing on top of it. Then he walked back to the bed and emptied the pitcher on top of the two criminals...

Confused, both of them sat up, looking at the two cops.

"Who are you?" Cash wanted to know.

"Don't you think that should be pretty obvious?" replied Stitch. "But seeing that you've asked: we're the police. And you are both under arrest for kidnapping a child..."

"Kidnapping?" the woman interjected. "What the hell...?"

"Sorry Mate!" she said, facing Cash. "This was not part of the deal, so I'm outta here..."

"Please take these handcuffs off me," she said to Bob. "I had nothing to do with this... uhm... kidnapping..."

"Sorry missy," replied Stitch. "You two are going to the police station to answer a few questions..."

"But I've told you th..." she began, but Stitch interrupted her.

"I know what you've told me," said Stitch. "And I don't believe you. Bob, get them their clothes..."

Bob nodded and collected two sets of clothes from the floor... he puts them on the bed...

The woman picked her clothes out of the pile and made for the bathroom.

"Stop!" commanded Stitch. "Not so fast. Where do think you're going?"

"On my way to get dressed," she replied, indicating the bathroom and then the clothes that were looking quite odd in her hands, given the fact that her hands were cuffed..."

"Fine." Agreed Stitch. "But leave the door open. I want to know when you try to escape through that bathroom window. And before you go, I'd like to know who you are. Name and social security no, please...?"

"I'm Dana Brush." She replied. Struggling a bit with her cuffed hands, she eventually succeeded pulling her ID Card from her coat pocket. She tossed it onto the bed.

"There you go," she said, facing the cops.

She disappeared into the bathroom, and came out about two minutes later, the sides of her top torn open so that she could fit it around her. Buttoned up, the top looked almost normal...

She walked to where a flabbergasted Cash was still lying. She gave him a tremendous punch to the face using both hands, considering the fact that she was handcuffed. Then she turned around, facing Stitch.

As if on second thought, she turned back to face Cash.

"Keep the cash!" she said. "I'm not interested in dirty money from a child kidnapper...!"

She turned back again, waiting...

"Are you done now?" Stitch asked the woman.

She snickered, then nodded.

Stitch read her rights, then handed her over to Bob.

"Finish the arrest of this freak," said Stitch, indicating Cash.

Bob read the criminal his rights, then threw him his pants after making sure that there were nothing of significance in the pockets. He found Cash's car keys and removed them.

"Get dressed," he ordered. "Unless you want to go to the police station in this condition...?"

Cash shook his head, took his pants and pulled it on as best he could with hands cuffed.

"What about my shirt?" Cash wanted to know.

Bob picked up the shirt from the floor and hung it around Cash's shoulders.

"That will have to do for now," said Bob. "You'll get the rest of your stuff when the crime investigation is done...

'Nasty, dirty, smelly shirt', thought Bob. Smells like dirt and nasty chemicals. Must have something to do with the drugs he'd probably forced that young girl to take...'

Cash fastened the top button on his shirt to keep it from falling on the floor.

Bob took Cash by his right arm and began to walk him out of the room. He indicated to the woman that she should fall in in front of them...

"When will I get my car keys back?" Cash wanted to know.

"Don't worry," replied Bob. "I'll hang on to them for a while. They'll be completely safe..."

Cash nodded.

"So," said Bob. What exactly did you want to do with that little girl?"

Silence.

"Okay," said Bob. "Take the 5th Amendment, if you like. There are methods to make someone like you talk..."

Cash just kept quiet.

9.15 pm

When they got to where the police cars were parked, Cash was shoved into one van and the doors closed with him inside.

The woman was shoved into the back of a squad car with bars between the back seat and the front cabin.

Everybody got in their respective cars. Cash and the woman were on their way to the cells, and Stitch and Bob drove to where Cash's vehicle was parked.

Bob locked the Anglia and put seals on the door handles and tape around the car. He also taped plastic over the broken window.

He then phoned for an officer to be sent out to guard the car through the night to make sure nobody interfered with the evidence...

Stitch and Bob went back into the motel to tape the door of the room shut for investigation. Stich went to the night manager to inform him of what's happened, and left his card with the man...

The rest of the officers went home. It was a long day, and they were tired...

*****

10.30 pm

Bob's phone rang. It was the hospital.

"Hi ma'am, said Bob. "How's the patient doing?"

"Hi officer," said the lady on the other side. "Could you and the Chief Commander please come and see us?"

"Now?" Bob wanted to know. "It's very late."

"Yes, officer, now," replied the lady. "It involves the patient, and it's very urgent..."

"Okay I'm on my way," said Bob and hung up.

He told Stitch about the lady's request.

"She sounded distressed," said Bob.

"Okay," said Stitch. "I'll go. You can either come with me, or go home. You won't be penalized if you choose to go home..."

"No problem, Chief." Replied Bob. I'm coming with you."

Stitch didn't say anything, but he clearly appreciated Bob's decision.

*****

10h50 pm

"Good evening, officers," said the nurse. "I'm so sorry for having had to request that you come here at this late hour."

"No problem at all, Ma'am," replied Stitch. "That's part of our duty..."

"All the same," she said. "I wish I didn't have to bring you this news..."

"What news, Ma'am?" Stitch wanted to know. "Did the little girl pass away?"

"No she didn't." replied the nurse. "But what had happened could turn out bad..."

She looked stressed.

"What happened Ma'am?" Bob wanted to know.

He felt that he had a special interest in her case, since he was the one to follow Cash's vehicle with her inside, then rescue her from the Anglia and then bring her to the hospital...

"She's vanished, Officer." Replied the nurse. "We were still attempting to revive her after drawing all those tubes of blood samples. We just went to have a cup of tea, and when we returned, she was gone...!"

"Gone!?" Interjected Stitch. "At what time did this happen?"

"Well," replied the nurse. "We discovered her disappearance at **10.23 pm**, just before I phoned your colleague..."

'Okay so much for going home.' He thought. "I won't be able to sleep until she's been found...!

Bob must have recognised the determined expression on Stitch's face.

"You're not going alone, Chief!" he said. I'm going with you. You can park your Merc, and we can go with my car..."

Relieved, Stich nodded.

"Thank you, Bob," he said. "I appreciate it..."

Chapter 16 – Captured and Escaped Again

Wenesday, September 14th, 1988

11.55 pm

Burinda had been running all the time since she'd managed to escape from the hospital. She was trying to reach her home.

'I'm so tired…' She thought. 'Cannot carry on… I need to rest…'

She stopped to look up at some street signs. One stated that Manhattan Beach was still five miles away. It was almost thirty when she'd started off. She'd come a long way… She didn't dare to stop now… She simply couldn't…

Burinda was taught from a very young age that determination can be your best friend when you are in any kind of danger

Burinda took off running again. She carried on and on…

At some point, she looked up and saw Manhattan beach in front of her…

"Oh! Thank goodness." She said to nobody in particular. "Another five minutes and I'll be home…!"

*****

Thursday, September 15th, 1988

6.30 pm

At last Burinda was home! She opened the gate and entered her garden…

'But why is everything so dark?' She wondered.

Slowly, she walked through the garden to the front door looking left and right several times to make sure nobody was around. Every tree and every shrub seemed to hide a moving shadow. It felt like ages before she eventually reached the door…

She opened the door and entered. Everything was dark…

Burinda stretched out her hand and switched on the light.

"Mom!" she called. "Daddy!"

No answer!

"Mom! Daddy!" Burinda tried again.

Suddenly, she remembered the giant of a man who'd run in the direction of her home when she'd run in the opposite direction at the school!

'Oh my gosh!' she thought, and panicked. 'I hope my parents are okay!'

Burinda walked from room to room, switching on the lights as she went. At last, all the lights in the house were on, and her parents were nowhere to be seen...

She decided to go to her bedroom and lock herself in while she waited for them to come home...

Burinda locked her bedroom door and sat down on her bed.

"I wonder what could've happened to them," she thought.

Suddenly, Burinda was feeling drowsy.

'What's that awful smell?' she wondered.

Try as she might, she couldn't keep her eyes open. Then all went black...

*****

Thursday, September 15th, 1988

7 pm

Burinda woke up, trying to determine where she was. She opened her eyes. She suddenly became aware that she was still on her bed, but that her hands and feet were tied...

She saw a man standing at the foot-end of the bed, but it wasn't the giant man that she'd encountered at the dance school.

The man was armed. He had a gun in his hand... He pointed the gun right at her.

'Why does he have a gun?' She thought. 'I wonder where the giant man is. What do these people want from me? Oh Daddy, where are you? I miss you so much!'

Burinda tried to get up, but to no avail. Besides the fact that she was tied to the bedframe, she couldn't even lift her head.

She began to cry.

"Why am I here?" she sobbed. "I can't do anything to you to hurt you. You are far too strong for me. I'd never be able to overcome you. Please just let me go? I want to go home…"

"Sorry, Girl," replied the man. "I cannot comply with your request…"

"Why not?" Burinda wanted to know.

"Instructions." Replied the man. "It's that simple…"

"Instructions from whom?" Burinda wanted to know.

"My boss," he replied. "If he was your boss, you would also be afraid to cross him…"

"Who's your boss?" she wanted to know. "Do I know him?"

Silence.

'Well perhaps he's not allowed to talk either,' thought Burinda.

"Are you allowed to untie me?" She asked, hopefully. "My blood circulation is cut off. Whatever you've tied me up with is hurting me and it's cutting off my blood circulation.

"I honestly don't know." He replied.

"Can you find out?" she asked.

He nodded.

"I will try." He replied.

Burinda had run out of questions to ask the thug.

He came closer to her and touched her face, studying it.

"What are you doing?" she wanted to know.

Silence.

Burinda looked at the man and saw that he was aiming the gun at her again.

'Oh no!' she thought. 'What is he doing? Am I going to die?'

He pulled the trigger, and a small dart hit her in the shoulder.

Suddenly, everything went black around her...

*****

Friday, September 16th, 1988

6 am

Burinda opened her eyes.

Everything around her looked strange.

"Where am I?" she wanted to know, but nobody was there to answer her question.

She sat up, looking around.

She was on a kind of an operating table.

Suddenly, she heard footsteps approaching. A door opened and she saw a woman approaching. The woman was wearing a mask and a surgical cap.

"Where am I?" Burinda asked. "And who are you?"

'I'm too scared to even look at anybody anymore,' she thought. 'I want my daddy. Oh Daddy, where are you?'

The woman removed her mask in order to speak to Burinda more clearly.

"Burinda," she declared. "I have arranged for you to be brought here so that I can alter your genetic structure. After that, you will be invincible as a ballet dancer. Nobody will ever be able to beat you on stage."

Burinda thought that she recognized the woman's voice, but she couldn't be sure...

"How do you know my name?" Burinda wanted to know. "And what does that mean... alter my genetic structure?"

"Look at me," said the woman. "I want this to sink in while I talk to you..."

She looked up, then sharply drew in her breath.

"What's wrong?" asked the woman, smirking. "You look as though you've seen a ghost..."

"You..." began Burinda, then started crying. "You are my science teacher! How could you do this to me?!"

She jumped off of the stainless steel table she was sitting on and took off, running to the door, but the woman ran after her and grabbed her arm.

"Give her a small dose of Ketamine, enough to calm her down," she said to the assistant, who'd just entered the room. "When we begin, we'll give her the full anesthetic."

"Right away, Professor," replied a female voice.

The professor aka science teacher dragged Burinda back to the operating table. Burinda struggled to get loose, but they held her down until the Ketamine IV had been attached to the vein in her arm. Slowly, she began to relax...

*****

6.30 am

The room had become a total blur. People were walking, but it seemed as though they moved in slow motion. Everything seemed clinically hygienic and everybody was wearing spotlessly white clothing.

All she could clearly see, was the determined expression in her science teacher's eyes, and the scalpel in the woman's hand.

The science teacher aka doctor looked up again, saying something to the assistant. Burinda couldn't make out any words at all.

Two hands gripped Burinda's upper arms and pushed her back so that she couldn't look at her science teacher, although she tried.

Suddenly, the woman looked like a monster to Burinda.

'I didn't even know that she was a doctor as well as a teacher...' Burinda thought. 'And come to think about it, I don't think she is either. She looks just like an alien to me...'

Burinda looked up again, seeing the scalpel getting closer... and closer... and closer... the masked face looked grotesque

'No!' she thought,' her drugged mind suddenly becoming clearer as her subconscious mind began to direct her conscious mind. 'I have to do something now! I cannot allow this to happen...'

A sudden surge of adrenaline coursed through her body as she sat up unexpectedly, and hit her science teacher's arm causing the scalpel to fall on the floor.

She pulled the hypodermic IV needle from her arm, jumped off of the operating table, ran to the door, opened it and charged out of the room, holding her arm where the needle was inserted and was just pulled out by herself. It was hurting, but she had no time to think about that...

"Wtf!" yelled the flabbergasted assisted, staring at her in unbelief. "She's not supposed to be able to do that!"

"Well don't just stand there," yelled the science teacher aka professor. "Follow her and bring her back!"

*****

6.35 am

Burinda found herself in a long passage. She chose a direction and ran. She passed an open door, ran through it and entered what looked like a mortuary, with about ten corpses lying on stainless steel tables with sheets over their heads. She silently closed the door behind her...

Then she heard footsteps coming down the passage.

'Oh my gosh!' she thought. 'I'd better do something quick!"

Frantically, she looked around her. One of the stainless steel tables appeared to be empty. She saw a sheet lying on top of it, though. She got onto the table and pulled the sheet over her head.

The door opened, and Burinda heard someone walk in.

"You're wasting your time!" she heard her science teacher yell. "All she's wearing is that thin surgical pinafore. She wouldn't last two minutes in here. Those corpses are all frozen. By now, she'd already be dead. I suggest you look in the other direction."

Burinda lay still, shivering profusely. She heard them exit the mortuary and walk down the passage, back to where they came from...

'She's right,' thought Burinda. 'I am dying of the cold in here. Somehow, I need to get out of here... fast! If I don't, I'll freeze solid in no time...'

She got off of the freezing cold table and walked to the door, which was still standing open. She slowly looked into the passage, in both directions. The passage was empty.

Burinda entered the passage and turned back in the direction she was going in when discovering the mortuary.

'I can't feel my legs,' she thought, creeping down the passage slowly, looking over her shoulder to confirm that she wasn't being followed...'

A little while later, she began feeling normal again as her temperature began to return to normal, and started running again. At the end of the passage, a door to her right was open. She looked in that direction and saw sunlight. She entered what seemed to be the reception area. She saw an open door, but she'd have to cross the lobby to get to it. It seemed to be the main entrance to the research center. Carefully, she looked around in the lobby. It seemed to be empty!

She ran outside after crossing the lobby and saw the main gate standing open. She began to run to the gate.

"Close the gate!" she heard her (now probably ex) science teacher yelling.

The gate began to close, but Burinda made it just in time. She was out in the street just before the gate locked.

Suddenly, the gate began to open again.

'Oh no!' thought Burinda. 'I'd better run for it before they catch me again!'

Burinda took off, and ran as fast as her 12-year-old legs could take her. Once again, she was determined not to let the danger of being recaptured a second time materialize… she had an excellent mentor in her father…

'Oh Daddy,' she thought, tears in her eyes. 'I do hope you are okay!'

Chapter 17 – Reunited and Justice for Burinda

Ten minutes later

Friday, September 16th, 1988

6.45 am

Burinda was still running. She kept looking back, but saw nobody following her.

'Perhaps they gave up looking for me,' she thought.

Fact of the matter was that they've considered it too risky to follow her, because of the high volume of traffic on that road.

Burinda was slowly but surely tiring out. She'd basically been running and fighting for survival since three days before, been drugged and under severe stress. She began to slow down.

She saw a police officer sitting in a car, inspecting his surroundings.

'Perhaps I should speak to him,' she thought. *'He should be able to help me.'*

She walked to the car.

"Excuse me, Officer," she addressed the man. "I think I urgently need help…"

Bob Binkley couldn't believe his eyes… and his luck! He and Stitch Quarry had been looking for this little girl ever since she'd vanished from the hospital three days before, and here she walked right up to him, asking for help…!

"Absolutely, little Girl!" he exclaimed. "We've been looking for you for the past three days! Your parents must be frantic! Where have you been?"

She began to cry.

"There there now young lady," Bob said. "Get in the car, then we can discuss this…"

"Actually," she said, "I'm not supposed to get into cars with strangers, Officer," she said. "It's because I got into a car with a stranger that I'm here, looking like this…"

She indicated the surgical pinafore that she was wearing.

"I don't even know where my clothes are." She said, pointing towards the research center. "They must still be somewhere in that building over there…"

"That's a good stance to take, little Girl" replied Bob. "But sometimes the only person who can help you offers you that help, and if you refuse to accept that help, you may land yourself in a dilemma as you've done this time. You got in a car with someone who was not your friend at all. "Next time you get in a car with someone you don't know, make sure that that someone is someone like me… a police officer… or a fire man… or a nurse… anyone wearing a uniform would be a good indication…"

She vigorously shook her head from side to side.

"Not a nurse!" she exclaimed as she fearfully looked in the direction of the research center. "Definitely not a nurse… and also not a teacher. Even if I know them…"

'Wonder what she's experienced inside that building to cause this fear of nurses,' he wondered. 'And what is this about teachers? Is there a teacher involved?'

He apprehensively looked in the direction of the research center.

"Well," he said. "Whatever the case may be, little girl, it's best to make sure about a person before you get into a car with them…"

"That's true, Officer," replied Burinda. "I got in that small silver car because I was scared. I was waiting for my daddy to pick me up, and he never came and his phone was off when I tried to call him. That man said he was going to fetch his little girl from horse riding lessons and then take me home, but instead he injected me with something and then I woke up in the hospital. I escaped, and I've been running ever since…"

"Yes I know you were taken to the hospital," said Bob, "since I was the one who took you there."

"You did?!" exclaimed Burinda, wide-eyed. "I mean, you were? I mean, *you* were the person who took me to the hospital? I thought it was that man who who'd injected that took me there, and that he was coming back for me. That's why I ran away from the hospital…"

"Yes, it was me who took you there," Bob confirmed. "The people at the hospital were trying to get the drugs out of your system that that man had injected into you. They found that the thug had injected a mixture of cocaine and heroine into your veins. I don't even know if you are aware of the danger of those drugs?"

"Yes, Officer," confirmed Burinda. "My daddy told me some. He always makes sure that I'm safe and that I know what to do and what not. I just freaked out a bit when he didn't pitch up at the dance school to pick me up. I'm sure he's okay… and my mom…"

"You don't have to be afraid of that freak anymore," said Bob. We took him into police custody and took him to the police station. He is in a cell right now, waiting to be booked for trial. We're gonna need your help to identify him, and we're gonna need a statement from you."

"I wouldn't mind doing that, Officer," Burinda declared. "Just as long as he won't see me there…"

"No, he won't be able to see you," Bob assured her. "But whatever the case may be, you'd better get in the car with me, since people are staring at you because of what you are wearing. I'll take you to your home where you can get into something more suitable. Then I'll take you to the police station where you can give us your statement and then identify the man who kidnapped you."

"Okay thank you Officer," said Burinda. "I don't mind getting in the car with you now that I know you better and I know you are a police officer and that you have rescued me on Friday night already."

Burinda saw a movement from the corner of her eye. She looked in that direction and saw a woman running towards her, waving her arms...

"Stop!" the woman yelled...

"Oh no!" exclaimed Burinda. "That must be one of the nurses looking for me!"

Bob started the car and Burinda got into the back of Bob's black Ford...

The car took off with a speed. Bob took Burinda to her home, and sent her inside to put on some proper clothes.

"I'll be waiting for you here." Said Bob. "Remember to put that pinafore you're wearing in a bag when you change, and bring it back to me. We're going to need it as evidence..."

"I will do that, Officer," she replied...

*****

Friday, September 16th, 1988

11 am

At the police station, Burinda was taken to a room where they took a statement from her to find out exactly what had happened to her.

Then blood samples were taken from her. They had to determine what type of drug she was injected with in the laboratory at the research center.

With the blood samples taken and given to the courier to take to the pathology department, Burinda was taken to a darkened room where she had to sit in front of a window that looked onto another, much smaller, brightly illuminated room, and wait for a number of men to walk into the smaller room so that she could identify the man who had kidnapped her. Bob and Stitch were with her in the room.

Six men walked into the smaller room on the other side of the mirror. Each man was carrying a number. They were numbered from 1 to 6.

"Don't worry," said Stitch. "He won't be able to see- or hear you at all. The other side of the window is a mirror..."

Relieved, she nodded.

Six men walked in and each of them was carrying a number. Bart was number 2. Burinda recognized him immediately.

"It was that man over there," said Burinda as she pointed towards him. "Number 2. That's the man who kidnapped me."

Bart squinted to try and see if he could see what was going on behind the mirror on his side, but to no avail. He couldn't see anything.

After the identification session, Burinda was taken to Stitch's office.

"I see your name is Burinda Davison?" inquired Stitch after reading her statement.

"Yes Sir, it is." Confirmed Burinda. "I don't live very far from here, only a few yards from the Manhattan Beach Pier. But I'm worried about my parents. I don't know where they are..."

Stitch's phone rang.

He answered the phone.

"Hi, this is Stitch." He said. "Talk to me..."

He listened a while.

"Ketamine, hey?" he said. "Poor girl had been heavily drugged since Friday..."

He listened again.

"Okay, he said after a while. "Let me know when they're here."

Then he hung up.

"Frankly, Burinda," he said. "You must be the most talked about elementary school kid in Manhattan, right now. After your parents came in to report you missing on Friday, just about everybody in your school began to look for you. Even your class mates…"

"My parents reported me missing?" asked Burinda, just to confirm that she'd heard him correctly…

"Yes." He replied. "Directly after what had happened to your dad…"

The phone rang again.

"Hi, this is Stitch." He said. "Talk to me…"

"Okay," he said after a few seconds. "Send them in."

"What happened to my dad, Officer?" Burinda asked, sounding concerned.

Then there was a knock on the door and it opened upon Stitch's direction…

"Why don't you ask him yourself?" he replied, pointing to the door…

Burinda looked up, then shrieked joyfully and jumped up.

"Daddy! Mommy!" she yelled, storming into her parents' open arms. The three remained in a family hug for about a minute, Burinda and her mom crying and Mr. Davison just hugging his girls tightly…

"Thank you Commander Quarry," said Mr. Davison. "Would it be okay if I took them home now?"

"No problem," replied Stitch. "Of course, there will be an investigation, and I will let you know if we need any more information from Burinda."

*****

As Burinda and her parents left the charge office, a young lady walked in.

A flash of semi-recognition spilled over Burinda's face. She tugged on her dad's sleeve.

"Quickly!" she exclaimed. "Let's get out of here, Daddy. Before she sees us..."

Section III – Grace

Chapter 18 - Getting to know the Research Centre

Grace Bronco had placed an advert in the paper to advertise her services as a surrogate mother.

Grace was lucky. The research center's agent had responded almost immediately by phoning her. He also agreed to pick her up at her home in Nevada, and bring her through to the research center...

*****

Wednesday, September 7th, 1988

9 am

Presently, Grace was sitting in the waiting room of the research center. Two other ladies were also there.

"Grace Bronco?" said a female voice.

Grace looked up. A woman was standing in the door.

Grace stood up.

"Yes?" she said.

"I am Professor Melissa Maitlon," said the woman. "Please follow me to my office..."

She turned around and began to walk down a long passage.

Grace followed the professor, who stopped at door No 4 and opened it.

"Could you enter please?" said the professor.

Grace complied...

Inside, the professor sat down behind a desk. She beckoned Grace to sit down on the empty chair across for her.

Grace sat down, facing the professor.

"What made you place an advertisement to become a surrogate mother, Grace?" the professor wanted to know.

"I think it was simply the fact that I need the money, professor." Replied Grace. "And of course, I would be an instrument in making a childless couple happy.

"Do I need any special qualifications Professor? Grace wanted to know."

"No, Grace," replied the professor, "Except that you need to be healthy and that that be nothing wrong with your reproductive abilities."

Grace seemed relieved.

"I can give you a positive on both, professor," said Grace. I am perfectly healthy and there is nothing wrong with my reproductive organs whatsoever."

"That's great, Grace." Said the professor. "Of course, we will do some tests before we do any procedures."

*****

Grace application was successful. She was offered 50000 US Dollars if she'd agree to be the surrogate mother for one of the research center's client couples, Mr. and Mrs. Laurient.

The research center also offered a substantial amount as a reward, if she agreed to have the procedure done at the research center and agreed to have some tests done prior to some extra procedures.

The proposed reward was 1 Million US Dollars, over and above her fee of 50000 US Dollars, which was payable by the couple whose baby she was to bear...

The only thing is, the entire procedure would have to be kept a secret, since surrogacy was illegal in New York, the state where the intended parents lived. And after birth, the baby would have to be registered as having been born out of the intended mother...

Grace had no problem with that, and neither did the intended parents.

As Grace understood it, she was about to become a surrogate mother for some childless couple's baby. The intended mother was infertile and the sperm of the father would be used to fertilize egg cells that would be taken from Grace's ovaries.

There's nothing new about being a surrogate mother, but the actual tests would involve altering the DNA of each of the embryos. The couple wanted the child to look like the intended mother, and to be exceptionally athletic, with a specific tendency towards ice skating in particular. The intended mother was a champion ice skater and wanted her children to follow in her footsteps...

An offer of a million US Dollars over and above the 50000 US Dollars offered by the intended parents wasn't an amount that anybody living in the 1970s would easily show away... especially if they had a large family, and jobs were scarce in their neighbourhood... so Grace had agreed to all of these procedures.

Actually, Grace had grabbed the opportunity with both hands.

*****

Wednesday, September 7th, 1988

2 pm

So presently, here she was, having reported at the reception desk, and having been referred to the research center waiting room. She'd reported for her first procedure... to donate her egg cells.

The only people waiting in the waiting room at the research center were Grace, and the Laurient couple whose child she was to bear. The couple had insisted that they be present during the entire procedure, from conception to birth, and they'd been introduced to Grace.

'I wonder how long this is still gonna take.' Wondered Grace...'

"Grace Bronco!" she heard her name.

"Yes?" said Grace, getting up from her seat.

She looked up into the formidable eyes of the professor's assistant, Shauna.

For a moment, Grace hesitated...

'What if something bad happens?' she thought

"Follow me," said Shauna. "We'll begin with a quick pap smear, just to make sure everything is okay with your reproductive organs."

Shauna didn't wait for Grace to actually follow her. She merely took Grace's arm gently, and began to walk.

'What the heck?' thought Grace. 'Does she have to do this? Couldn't she just wait for me to follow?'

But Grace kept her thoughts to herself and made a firm decision to stop worrying about the program. She just followed where Shauna dragged her...

'In nine months all of this will be over,' thought Grace, 'and me and my family will be out of our financial trouble..."

*****

Thursday, September 8th, 1988

9 am

"Grace," said Shauna. "Why don't you go into room No 4 and change into the clothes provided?"

Grace nodded, and opened the door to No 4. It was empty, except for a tray on wheels that contained some instruments, an array of machines and an examination table on top of which she found a flimsy cotton pinafore and a pair of disposable paper slippers.

After removing her own clothes, she changed into the pinafore and the slippers, and then waited.

A man entered the room.

"Hi Grace, I am professor Maitlon," he greeted and introduced himself. "You may get onto the table and lie down."

Grace complied.

"Now," he continued. "Do you have any question, before we begin?"

"Yes, Professor," she replied. "I would just like to know if the DNA changes to the embryos will have any adverse effect on them… or me…?"

"No, not at all," he lied. "DNA manipulation had been developed onto an exact science. We locate the particular genes that need to be altered or replaced, and voila. The baby will display the related attributes."

"I am relieved," replied Grace. "At some point, I was in doubt."

"No need to be concerned about anything whatsoever," he reassured her. "Is there anything else?"

"No," she replied. "You may go ahead and do the pap smear. Is it going to hurt?"

"Not more than a tiny prick." He said. "If you wish, we can give you a local anesthetic?"

She shook her head.

"Not necessary," she replied. "I'm sure I'll survive…"

He nodded, smiling.

The procedure took about 10 minutes, during which he took a tiny sample of her cervix.

"Okay, I'm done," he said. "You may change back into your own things now. While you do that, I'll go and process the smear. Once you're done, please wait for me in the waiting room…"

She nodded.

*****

Grace's pap smear was normal, so they could go ahead with the procedures.

Since a woman usually produces only one egg cell per month, Grace was given fertility drugs to stimulate egg cell production in order for her to produce several egg cells for the procedure that she was about to participate in. During this period, the research center provided free accommodation for Grace on the premises, so that Shauna could monitor the process to determine the best time for the egg cells to be extracted.

Presently, Grace as well as the Laurient couple were in the waiting room. Grace was ready for her egg cells to be extracted.

'Well,' thought Grace. 'This is it. If, for any reason, I have second thoughts, this is my last chance to voice it...'

"Grace," she heard her name.

She looked up and saw Shauna indicating that she should follow her. This time, they walked down a long passage until they came to a closed door.

Shauna opened the door and stepped inside, indicating that Grace should follow her.

Grace followed Shauna, entering what looked like a laboratory. There was what looked like an operating table in the center of the floor, an odd-looking piece of machinery next to it. There were also a tray on wheels containing some instruments.

"Same drill," said Shauna. Change into the provided clothes, then get onto the table.

Grace looked apprehensively at the machine next to the table...

"That is just a monitor that the professor attaches to the ultrasound probe so that he can see where the egg cells are so that he can safely extract them without damaging them." Explained Shauna. "The probe is that instrument right there next to the monitor, and its technical name is a Transvaginal Ultrasound Transducer. It is a suction device that is fitted with a thin needle called an aspiration needle, through which the egg cells will be pulled when he extracts the egg cells from the ovaries and from the follicle sacks that are attached to the ovaries. The egg cells, together with their surrounding follicle fluid, will be sucked into the egg cell collection tube, which is fitted with a suction pump. Once we have all the available egg cells in the collection tube, and the clips removed that were used to seal the fallopian tubes to prevent them guiding any egg cells into the uterus, the procedure will be over."

"Interesting." Said Grace.

But she just listened although she didn't really understand all the terms. She just wanted the procedure to be over...

Professor Maitlon walked into the laboratory.

"Hello, Grace?" he greeted. "How are you doing?"

"I'm a bit scared, Professor," replied Grace. "Last night, I had a nightmare in which the babies were all born and were attacking me because I've allowed their DNA to be altered. I know it was just a dream, but still. It was a nightmare..."

"That's 100% normal, Grace." Replied Professor Maitlon. Nine out of ten surrogate mom's get these nightmares..."

"It's still not very nice," said Grace. "Have you ever had cases where the in vitro had complications?"

"No not at all," replied Professor Maitlon. "But lets get this done, so that you can go to your room and rest. I have arranged for you to stay on until the actual implantation of the embryos..."

"That's nice of you Professor," replied Grace.

He gave her a sedative to keep her calm during the procedure, as well as a pain killer to prevent her experiencing pain.

Grace was conscious the whole time, and able to see how the egg cells were being pulled out of her ovaries and the follicles that were attached to the ovaries.

Once the procedure was over, Grace was taken to her room. Shauna put her to bed, and let her sleep.

*****

Friday, September 9th, 1988

9 am

Professor Maitlon took the newly collected egg cells to his research laboratory where they were placed into a fertilization bowl. Mr. Laurient's sperm was ready by the time the professor reached the laboratory.

There were eight egg cells collected, and the sperm count was good enough to successfully fertilize all eight.

The altered DNA was introduced.

The embryos were placed in a freezing unit, ready and waiting to be inserted into Grace's uterus.

*****

Grace woke up the next morning.

Relieved that the egg cell extracting procedure was over, she decided to take it easy for the next 5 days while the DNA procedures would take place, and she would just wait for the next procedure in which she would be involved, being the actual insemination of the embryos into her uterus...

*****

Wednesday, September 14th, 1988

9 am

"Grace," she heard her name.

She looked up, and saw Shauna standing in her bedroom door.

"Yes, Shauna?" she replied. "Is it time?"

"Yes, Grace." Said Shauna. "Please follow me. Professor Maitlon wants to discuss your embryo implantation."

"Okay," replied Grace. "But is this not a bit early?"

"Yes," replied Shauna. "This will just be a consultation. The actual procedure has been scheduled for the day after tomorrow, when all the tests will be finalized."

"Okay no problem." Agreed Grace. "Shall we go then?"

"Yes," said Shauna. "Let's go."

As always, Shauna took Grace's arm and began to walk

'I wonder why she always does this,' thought Grace like I'm some kind of prisoner..."

*****

9.30 am

Grace was sitting in Professor Maitlon's office, in a chair across from him, waiting to hear what he had to say.

"Well, Grace," he said. "It's almost time."

Grace smiles nervously.

"Is there anything specific that I need to know about this procedure, Professor?" She wanted to know. From what I understand, it's quite a painless, simple procedure that can be done with me being awake?"

"Only one thing, Grace." He replies. "I am going to implant all eight embryos, since we are not sure whether any of the potential babies will actually survive. But there is also a chance of all eight surviving. Just so that you are aware. Get ready for life in abundance, since it may so work out that you will be giving birth to eight babies, after carrying them full term..."

For a few seconds, Grace just stared at him. Wondering whether she was misunderstanding.

'How could he expect this of me?' she thought. 'I don't think I have to do this...!'

"What's wrong, Grace?" he wanted to know. "You look a bit overwhelmed?"

"Oh my gosh, you must be joking!" exclaimed Grace. "Are you sure that that's such a good idea? What if all eight actually attach and survive? Surely I wouldn't be able to carry eight babies full term? Considering my weight, such a pregnancy might very well kill me!"

His facial expression became rigid. The sudden look of solid crystal in his ice blue eyes sent a chill down her spine.

Then his face relaxed, and he smiled his usual smile. But for the first time since she'd met him, she actually looked him in the eye when he smiled and a second chill went down her spine.

'Oh my gosh!' she thought. 'I never noticed this before, but his smile doesn't reach his eyes! It's like they are empty! Dead, and empty. This man doesn't feel anything for anybody but himself!'

"May I please think about this and give you answer tomorrow?" she inquired."

Somehow, she didn't think that delayed her answer would anything, but she was playing for time...

"Come now, Grace," replied the professor. "You'll be surprised at what the human uterus is capable of doing." There have been cases reported of women successfully carrying and giving birth to eight, nine and ten babies at the same time, all of them surviving. I could give you url links to all of those cases, so that you can look them up on the internet. Would you like me to do that...?"

'I might as well let him give me those links.' She thought. 'Somehow, I don't think I will leave his office alive if I'd refuse...'

"Sure, Professor," she replied, smiling. "I'd love to look those up."

And somehow, for the first time in her life of twenty three years, she realized that she, also, was smiling a smile that didn't reach her eyes. But her smile wasn't chilling to the bone like his. Her smile was just an empty muscle action in an expressionless face, because it was born out of fear...

He smiled his chilling smile again.

"That's my girl!" he said "I knew you'd come to your senses!"

He wrote something on a sheet of paper, then hands the sheet to her. His hand momentarily touched hers, causing her to shiver. His hand was ice cold...

'Why on Earth didn't I ever notice this about him?' she wondered. 'It's as though he's not human at all! Is it possible that the prospect of earning a large amount of money could've dulled my senses this much?'

"Thank you professor," she said and her voice sounded different to her... kind of 'mechanical...

She stood up to leave his office.

"You're welcome Grace," he said. "So I will see you tomorrow, then?"

"Absolutely, professor," she replied. "I'm sure I will have a positive answer for you tomorrow..."

Grace opened the door and left the professor's office. As if on cue, Shauna was waiting for her directly outside of the door. Grace looked at Shana as she smiled. Grace then realized, suddenly, that Shauna, like the professor, had the same, kind of crystalline, smile that never reached her eyes. For the second time that day, someone had sent a bone-chilling shiver down her spine...

"Okay," said Shauna. "Let's go..."

Shauna took Grace by the arm, as she always did. Previously, it didn't bother her that much. But this time, it induced fear...

Chapter 19 - Reconsideration

Thursday, September 15th, 1988

9 am

Everything within Grace was protesting after she had linked to the websites that Professor Maitlon had given her to look into.

'I really don't think that I want the professor to place all eight embryos in my uterus.' She thought. 'I am quite certain that the female human body was never meant to experiment on like this. Neither do I think that the female human body was meant to carry and/or deliver more than two or three babies at the same time. The norm is one, and that is what I had signed up for. Definitely not eight. I am quite sure that my body would not be able to take that, and I think I want to cancel this deal...'

"Are you ready to go?" Shauna wanted to know.

Grace looked up, and saw Shauna standing at her bedroom door.

'The woman really does a way of sneaking up on a person...' thought Grace. That's uncanny and I am not comfortable with the fact that she's all around me on a 24/7 basis...'

"Go where?" Grace wanted to know.

"You did say you would give the professor your answer today, didn't you?" inquired Shauna.

"How so you know about that, Shauna?" Grace wanted to know.

"Well," continued Shauna. "Did you?"

"Well, yes," confirmed Grace. "But that was between him and me. Did you eavesdrop, by any chance?"

Shauna didn't answer the question.

"Okay," said Shauna. "You've confirmed that you'd arranged with to give him your answer today, so let's go...!"

As usual, Shauna lightly took Grace by the arm and began to walk. This irritated Grace and she wanted to pull her arm from Shauna's grip, but Shauna tightened her grip and continued walking, increasing her speed. Grace was compelled to follow…

*****

Friday, September 16th, 1988

8 am

Once again, Grace was facing Professor Maitlon in his office.

"So Grace," the professor wanted to know, his ice cold fish-like eyes upon her. "Do you have a suitable answer for me?"

'I wonder what he means by 'suitable,' wondered Grace. 'Somehow, I do not think that he would be satisfied with a 'no…'

She kept her thoughts to herself…

"Professor," she said. "I have consulted those websites, and it's all well and good. But those women were huge before they actually gave birth to those masses of babies. The websites don't state whether their bodies have actually returned to normal… or what their lives were like after they gave life to those babies. Yes, they got their names in the Guinness Book of Records, but were they happy after that? Or did they feel like people were considering them to be freaks?"

"Is that your final answer?" he wanted to know.

"I haven't given you an answer yet, Professor." She replied. "I've asked you some questions. Were those women able to lead normal after the births of those children? Did their bodies return to normal?"

"I don't know, Grace." He replied. But that's not the issue here."

"What is the issue, Professor" Grace wanted to know.

"The issue is that you have tied yourself to an agreement, and the Laurients expect you to honor that agreement."

"I'm prepared to honor the agreement, Professor," replied Grace. "But the agreement was for one baby. Not eight."

"Okay," replied the professor. "Would you consider doing this if they'd agree to pay you 50000 US Dollars for each surviving baby?"

'Not on your life will I agree to more than one baby,' thought Grace. 'But who knows what might happen to me if I'd tell him that?'

She nodded.

"Yes, Professor," she replied. "I will consider that, but to a maximum of four embryos being implanted in my uterus. Eight are simply too many. They wouldn't have to pay me for the number of embryos, but for the number of surviving babies after they'd been born..."

The professor's ice cold eyes settled on her once again.

"I think you are worried about minor little things, Grace." replied the professor. "Chances are that only 50% or less of the embryos would actually attach and be born eventually. Also, consider the fact that you will be cared for by us. We... I... will be here for you all the time, since you will be taken care of here, at the **MaitlonByTwo Research Center** for the entire term."

'The thought of that happening, scares me more than any other,' thought Grace. I think the time had come for me to reconsider. Most of all, the time had come for me to leave this premises and insist that they doe the procedure at a normal hospital.'

Grace realized that telling him her thoughts could prove to be fatal, so she just shrugged.

"Okay," she said, smiling. "You have convinced me. So let's give it a shot and see what happens..."

"That's my girl," replied Professor Maitlon. "So shall we go to the laboratory?"

Grace frowned.

"You said the procedure would take place tomorrow?" she inquired. "I don't think that, mentally, I am quite ready yet. I need to prepare myself mental, emotionally and psychologically."

He nodded.

"Okay, fine." He said. "I will see you in the laboratory at 11 Am tomorrow. Until then..."

"Thank you Professor, said Grace and stood up to leave his office.

"You're welcome Grace," he said. "So I will see you tomorrow, then?"

"Absolutely, professor," she replied. "I'm sure I would have worked through my issues by then..."

Grace opened the door and left the professor's office.

Again, as if on cue, Shauna was waiting for her directly outside of the door.

Grace looked at Shauna as she smiled. Again, she felt that chill running down her spine...

'What is it with these people?' Grace wondered. They all have this chilling smile that doesn't reach their empty, crystalline, eyes.'

Almost involuntarily, she looked at Shauna's eyes... and for the second time, the look of Shauna's eyes had sent a bone-chilling shiver down her spine...

"Okay," said Shauna. "Let's go..."

Once again, she took Grace by the arm, as she always did. And once again, instead of being reassuring, it induced fear...

"Shauna," said Grace. "Would you please stop doing that..."

"Doing what?" Shauna wanted to know.

"Please stop taking my arm every time we walk somewhere together." Replied Grace. "It makes me feel like I'm a captive and that I'm not allowed to go anywhere besides when I'm with you..."

Shauna just looked at Grace, but didn't respond to Grace's request...

Chapter 20 – Chilling Revelation

Saturday, September 17th, 1988

5.30 am

Grace woke up earlier than normal, and was out in the passage to go to the bathroom.

'Might as well get ready before the drill sergeant gets here,' she thought. 'That way, I might avoid being tagged along like a prisoner...'

As she was about to turn the corner in order to enter the bathroom, her eye caught an open door that she'd never seen before because it was always closed.

She decided to investigate the room that the open door led to.

Grace entered the room.

'Wow!' she thought. I'll freeze to death in here! Why would they have such a cold room?'

Grace looked around, and to her horror, she saw several stainless steel tables on top of which were what appeared to be corpses covered by sheets.

Then she heard footsteps as if someone was approaching fast, running barefoot.

She hid behind a large cupboard, which she then realized most probably also contained corpses, since it had drawers similar to what would be found in a proper mortuary.

From behind the cupboard, she saw a young girl of about 12 years old enter the room, looking around. The girl was dressed only in a pair of paper slippers and a surgical pinafore...

The girl seemed to be terrified of something, or someone.

Once again, she heard footsteps approaching fast. It sounded like two people running.

The young girl frantically looked around, then spotted an empty table with only a sheet on top. She ran to the empty table, climbed onto it and covered herself with the sheet.

Suddenly, someone entered the room.

Grace couldn't believe her eyes. I was Shauna entering, looking around. Could she have been chasing the child?

After what had transpired the last two days, Grace thought that it was quite possible.

"You're wasting your time!" Grace heard Professor Maitlon yell as he entered the room. "All she's wearing is that thin surgical pinafore. She wouldn't last two minutes in here. Those corpses are all frozen. By now, she'd already be dead. I suggest you look in the other direction."

Shauna looked around for another few seconds, then both of them exited the room. Grace heard both of them run back to where they came from...

A few seconds later, Grace saw the young girl get off of the table and slowly walk out of the room, shivering from the cold...

'Shit, he's right,' she thought. I'll die of the freezing temperature in here. I think this is, indeed, a mortuary. Somehow, I need to get out of this research centre... like yesterday! The police need to know what's going on in this evil place...'

Grace got up, and began to walk. Suddenly, she heard someone else approaching, walking carefully, as if sneaking. Grace ducked behind a curtain hanging from the wall.

However, the person didn't enter the mortuary.

Grace left her hiding place and continued walking, exiting the mortuary.

'I'd better not go in the same direction as Shauna and the professor,' she thought...'

She began to walk in the opposite direction

"Pssst!" Someone tried to draw her attention.

Grace looked in the direction from which the sound was coming, and saw a girl of about 18 years old standing in an open doorway. Suddenly, the girl grabbed her arm and pulled her into the room, closed the door and locked it behind them.

The girl indicated the she should be quiet...

"Hi!" she whispered. "I'm Grace. "Are you also a victim of this research center?"

Judy spent the next few minutes to Grace how to find the exit and escape...

Chapter 21 – Escape

Saturday, September 17th, 1988

7 am

Grace exited Judy's room and entered the passage. She walked in the direction indicated by Judy.

'I'd better be careful now,' she thought, creeping down the passage. They will quite easily kill me... I'd better keep my eyes and ears and my sixth sense open. Cannot afford to be caught right now.'

She looked back over her shoulder, but saw nothing. Slowly, but surely, she approached the end of the passage.

When she'd reached the end of the passage, she looked to her right, as described by Judy. She saw the lobby, and the open door. She walked into the lobby. Carefully, she looked around. The lobby seemed to be empty!

She crossed the lobby, saw the gate remote switch as described by Judy and pushed it. The gate began to open, and Grace began to run to the gate.

"Close the gate!" she heard the voice of Professor Maitlon, yelling.

The gate began to close, but Grace is, in fact a fast runner and made it in good time. She was out in the street and well on her way down the street before the gate eventually closed.

'I'd better run for it.' Grace thought. ' Don't want them to catch me!'

Grace took off, and ran as fast as she could, looking around to see if she could spot a police officer.

"About thirty yards ahead of her, she saw a little girl that she saw in the center mortuary earlier, climb into a police car.

"Wait!" she yelled. "Stop! I also need help!"

But the police car already took off.

Grace frantically looked around.

'There should be another police officer here somewhere,' she thought.

Determination took hold of her.

'If it's the last thing I do,' she thought, 'I WILL get to the police to report this. Those people cannot be allowed to get away with what they are doing...!"

Grace began to walk, looking around to see if she could spot another police officer. Fortunately, the shoes she was wearing were rather comfortable...

Grace kept walking, until she came to a large green park that had lots of vegetation and where little kids were playing.

'I'm so tired.' She thought. 'Better just rest a while.'

The park looked safe enough, so she decided to rest in the park. She walked through the open gate and spotted a park bench which were well hidden from the street by shrubs.

Grace sat down. And then emotion took over and she began to cry.

"Daddy," she heard a little kid's voice. "I wonder why that lady is crying…"

A few seconds later, someone touched her shoulder. She looked up and saw a man standing in front of her, holding the hand of a little boy.

"Excuse me, Ma'am," said the man. "I am Duke Draper. My little boy just made me aware that you were crying. Are you okay? Do you need some help?"

She looked at him, wondering whether she should trust him

'He looks quite harmless,' she thought. 'Especially with a little kid holding his hand. And I did hear the kid calling him 'Daddy.' And yes, I do need help…'

"Yes, Sir, thank you for asking," replied Grace. "My name is Grace Bronco and I do need help, urgently."

"What kind of help do you need, Grace?" Duke wanted to know.

She felt her tears coming back, but suppressed them.

'I cannot afford not getting the help I need because of a lot of irritating sobs and tears…' she thought…

"I urgently need to get to a police station to report a serious crime." She replied. "I'm not from around here, so I don't even know where to begin. I've been walking around, searching for close to two hours now. I'm terrified that the people who are chasing me might find me before I find a police station…"

"Well, Grace," said Duke. "You are in luck. I am about to take my little boy back to the after school care center. I am willing to take you to the police station and drop you off before I drive to the after school care center. Would that be okay with you?"

Grace heaved a sigh of relief.

"Yes, it will indeed be okay with me, thank you so much, Duke!" she said. "I appreciate this more that you'll ever know!"

"You're welcome, Grace." Replied Duke, and pointed towards a yellow cab that was parked close to the gate. "My car is over there."

"A cab?" she inquired.

"Don't worry," he said. "It's on me. I won't charge you."

"That is so nice of you!" exclaimed Grace. How can I ever repay you?"

"Not necessary," he replied, smiling. "It will be my good deed for the day. Doing my part for the community, and teaching my son how to be human."

He smiled at his son.

"Shall we go, little Duke?" he asked his son.

The boy smiled and nodded affirmatively.

"Yes, Daddy," he replied. "The lady needs help, so let's help her..."

The three of them walked to the cab. When they got there, Duke unlocked the doors and little Duke took the front passenger seat. Grace got in the back of the cab.

Grace began to tell Duke about what had happened at the research center, but he stopped her.

"The less I know, the better," he explained. "Absolutely the only thing I need to know, is that I've dropped off a lady at the police station who needed help. Anything else, will come on the news... if it's gonna reach the main stream media. If not, then so be it."

"Somehow, I agree with you," replied Grace. "Just know that I'll be forever grateful to you."

"It will always remain a pleasure to help someone in need." He said as he stopped.

"Here we are," he continued, pointing to the main entrance gate of the police station. "Go through the gate, and up the steps, and you'll get to the charge office. The Chief commander is Stitch Quarry. He is a personal friend of mine..."

"Thank you so much, Duke," said Grace. "Perhaps, someday, I could return the favor. I live in Nevada, but who knows?"

Grace closed the cab door and waved Duke and his son off...

Chapter 22 – Justice for Grace

Saturday, September 17ᵗʰ, 1988

10 am

Grace was lucky to meet Duke, else she would have had to continue looking for the police station since she was not from the Los Angeles area. She would certainly have found it eventually, but valuable time would've been lost.

She got out of Duke's cab and welcomed the sight of the blue light at the gate.

She walked through the gate, and climbed the few steps to door, as Duke said she should. She briefly noticed a couple and their little girl of about 12 years old walking down the steps.

The little quickly looked away when she noticed Grace, pulled on her father's sleeve and urgently whispered something. The man looked at Grace, nodded and protectively put his arm around the little gitl's shoulders...

Grace frowned.

'Now where do I know this little girl from?' Grace wondered, having no idea at the time that she would get to know the little girl, Burinda, a lot closer not too much later.

Grace walked through the main entrance to the police station and entered the charge office. She walked up to the service desk in the charge office, and waited.

"Good afternoon, Ma'am," greeted the officer behind the desk. "How do we help you today?"

"Good afternoon, Officer," replied Grace. "I need to urgently speak to Chief Commander Stitch Quarry. Nobody else will do, since I need to report a serious crime and some of the info may be classified."

"Are you from around here, Ma'am?" the officer wanted to know.

"No officer." Replied Grace. "I'm from Nevada."

"May I have your name, please Ma'am?" Requested the officer.

"Sure," said Grace. "My name is Grace Bronco."

"One moment, Ma'am," said the officer. "I'm calling the Chief Commander right away."

"Thank you Officer," she replied.

The Officer dialled a number.

"Hi Chief," he said into the receiver. "We have a Grace Bronco who wants to see you. She needs to report a serious crime."

"Right away, Chief!" he said after a while. Then he hung up.

"Please follow me, Ma'am," he said. "Commander Quarry is waiting to see you."

Grace followed the officer down a short passage and knocked on a door displaying the name "Ron Quarry."

'Wonder where he got the nickname 'Stitch' from...' she thought...

"You may enter," called Stitch.

The officer opens the door and indicates to Grace that she should enter.

"Thank you, Officer," said Grace and walked into Stitch's office.

"Hi Grace," greeted Stitch, indicating the open chair across from him. "I'm Stitch. Please take a seat."

"Thank you, Commander," said Grace and sat down, facing Stitch.

"Forgive me, Commander," she inquired. "I'm... just wondering where you got the nickname 'Stitch' from?"

"Not at all, Grace," he replied.

He rolled up his left sleeve and pointed to a very small scar precisely on top of his elbow.

"See this scar?" he wanted to know.

She nodded.

"It's difficult, but I see it..." she replied.

"Well I'm surprised that you do," he replied. "I got the wound when I elbowed a crook who tried to escape. It earned me exactly on stitch, and my men found it so funny that they started calling me 'Stitch.' I kinda liked the idea so adopted the nickname..."

Then he smiled...

"I believe you have something to tell us, Grace?" inquired Stitch.

"Yes, Commander," confirmed Grace, smiling back. "Actually, I have quite a lot to tell you."

"Please go right ahead, Grace." Said Stitch.

For a moment Grace looked as though she couldn't find her words.

"Wow, I'm not sure where to begin," she then said.

"Why don't you start at the beginning?" suggested Stitch.

"Okay," said Grace. "Here goes. It all began when I placed an advertisement in the newspaper, advertising myself to be a surrogate mother for a childless couple."

"An agent of the **MaitlonByTwo Research Center** called me and we met up to discuss the issue.

"The agent, I think he said his name was Bart, said that I was the perfect candidate for a client couple of the research center. He said the match was spot on, and he arranged to take me there."

"Grace," inquired Stitch, "This... Bart. What model of car did he drive?"

"It was a silver car," replied Grace. "I think... it was some kind of a Ford. I saw the Ford logo on it. Not sure what model of Ford, though..."

"Could it have been a Ford Anglia?" Stitch suggested.

"I'm really not sure." Replied Grace. But I think I'd recognize it if I should see it."

Stitch picked up a folder and opened it. He paged through the documents in the folder and pulled out a photograph.

"Is this the car?" he inquired, handing her the picture.

Grace carefully looked at the picture.

"I couldn't positively state beyond any doubt that this is the car," she replied. "But if it's not then it looks exactly like that car of Bart's."

"I think that's enough to get you to do an identification of the person we have in custody, Grace." Said Stitch. "Would you be prepared to do that?"

"Yes, Commander." Replied Grace. "I will do that with pleasure."

"Great!" said Stitch. "We are having a session in an hour from now. Would that suit you?"

Grace nodded.

They continued doing Grace's statement.

"What happened after Bart had taken you to the research center, Grace?" Stitch wanted to know.

"I was interviewed by a woman, Professor Melissa Maitlon." replied Grace. "She told me more or less what would have been expected of me."

"And then?" Stitch wanted to know.

"And then," replied Grace," I've had to complete an application form."

"Was that an application form to become a surrogate mother?" inquired Stitch.

"Yes, Commander, replied Grace. "It was."

"And when did you hear back from the center?" asked Stitch.

"Three days later." Replied Grace. "A nurse by the name of Shauna called me to let me know that my application had been approved. And the next day, Bart came to pick me up at my home in Nevada."

"When did you begin to have second thoughts about the deal?" Stitch wanted to know.

"On the very first day already," replied Grace. "The nurse, Shauna, asked me to follow her to the laboratory. But she didn't allow me to follow her… she took me by the arm and literally marched me to the lab. Then, when I got to the lab, the person who did the procedure was a man, Professor Rudolph Maitlon. " I was under the impression that it would've been done by his wife, Professor Melissa Maitlon. That came as a bit of a shock, and I felt like cancelling, but Professor Rudolph Maitlon has a way of coercing one into doing what he wants one to do, even if it's against ones better judgment…"

"I see." Said Stitch." Is there anything else at all that you feel we should know, Grace?" Stitch wanted to know.

"Yes," replied Grace. "They have a mortuary containing several deep frozen corpses. I ran into it quite by accident just this morning. That's what's made me finally decide to leave the place and get to the police as fast as I could…"

"And how did you manage to get out?" Stitch wanted to know.

"I had help from a woman called Judy Maitlon," replied Grace. "Without her, I'd probably be dead right now…"

"Okay," said Stitch. "That will be all for now."

Stitch stood up.

"Could you please follow me, Grace?" requested Stitch. "I would like us to do that identification session now."

Grace nodded.

"No problem, Commander," she said.

Saturday, September 17th, 1988

1 pm

Stitch took Grace to a darkened room where she had to sit in front of a window that looked into another, much smaller, brightly illuminated room. They waited for a number of men to walk into the smaller room so that she could identify the man who had picked her up from her home in Nevada and had brought her to the **MaitlonByTwo Research Center**.

Stitch remained in the room with her.

Six men walked into the smaller room on the other side of the mirror. Each man was carrying a number. They were numbered from 1 to 6. Bart was number 4. Grace recognized him immediately.

"Don't worry," said Stitch. "He won't be able to see- or hear you at all. The other side of the window is a mirror..."

Relieved, she nodded.

It was that man over there," said Grace as she pointed towards Bart. "Number 4. That's the man who picked me up from my home in Nevada and brought me to the research center."

Section IV – Arrest and Justice

Chapter 23

Monday, September 19th, 1988

10 am

Arrest – Shauna

Stitch parked his car two blocks away from the **MaitlonByTwo Research Center**. Three squad cars stopped behind him.

His cell phone rang and he answered it.

"Hi!" he said into the receiver. "This is Stitch. Talk to me!"

"Hi Chief!" replied Bob. "Everything is ready my side. Just give the word, and we'll take them out..."

"Great!" said Stitch. "Just waiting for the van to arrive..."

As if on cue, the police van stopped behind the convoy.

"Okay, Bob!" said Stitch. The van is here. Take them out!"

Bob and three other officers got out of the two cars behind Stitch, who was in the process of getting out of his Merc when they saw the gate of the research center open.

Stitch held up his hand.

A midnight blue Volvo with tinted windows came driving out of the research center yard, followed by a cold storage van.

"Go guys!" yelled Stitch. "It seems the spider is abandoning the web...!"

All five police vehicles took off, sirens on and blue lights flashing, and began to follow the research center's vehicles. The research center vehicles flew up Hawthorne Boulevard. The police vehicles all followed hot on the tails of the perpetrators' vehicles.

All the vehicles moving like crazy from the research center, they had just turned from Hawthorne Boulevard onto the fast lane of

W-190th Street, decidedly picking up speed. The police vehicles, with sirens on and blue lights flashing, resembled a typical police-escorted motorcade, except, they did not have flags and all the police vehicle were following, none of them leading....

Speeding at top speed in a light shower of rain, the tires of the Merc singing on the asphalt, Stitch thanked his lucky stars that the Merc had just been serviced, and had just been equipped with brand new tires and brake pads.

Stitch talked on the radio:

"Okay Guys, seems like they're headed for the Nevada/California border post," he said. "Looks Like they're moving in the direction the I-15. They'd obviously planned for at least a ten hour drive before crossing into Nevada, and it's our job to prevent them from crossing. Flash your head lights if you're copying..."

All the police headlights flashed...

"Great!" Said Stitch. "Let's do this, then...!

The research centre vehicles stayed ahead of the police vehicles for a while, but then the cold storage truck seemed to fall back.

"The Volvo is charging like mad," came Stitch's voice on the air, "but we should be able to stop the cold storage van soon. It seems to be falling back rapidly. I've already let the Nevada Police Dept know, so they are ready for the Volvo, just in case. Just keep an eye out for anything fishy..."

"Copy that Chief," came several voices in reply..."

"Great, Guys," said Stitch. "Bob, you take the lead following the Volvo. Take one of the other vehicles with you. The rest of us will cling to the cold storage vehicle. I'm quite inquisitive as to what we'll find in there."

His words were barely spoken, when the cold storage vehicle suddenly turned onto Avalon Blvd.

Stitch followed immediately, as did his two companion vehicles. The police vehicles clung to the cold storage vehicle and was closing the distance fast when, suddenly, the driver of the cold storage vehicle lost control of the vehicle, hit a large boulder on the center island on Avalon Blvd, directly across the Dr. Martin Luther King Jr. Library on the center

The vehicle overturned and landed on its side next to the boulder it hit...

All six police officers from the three police vehicles jumped out of the cars. Two of them immediately cordoned off the road in both directions, signalling to the oncoming traffic to turn around.

Stitch and two other officers got busy setting the driver of the cold storage vehicle free. This took them approximately 30 minutes, but eventually the police had Shauna Lucas in custody, having loaded her in the back of the police van.

The cold storage van was confiscated in the name of national security, and the contents transferred to the premises of the FBI for further investigation. The vehicle was impounded and Shauna was booked into the police holding cell.

After all of these procedures were finalized, all vehicles took off again, following the trail of the Volvo. Bob kept Stitch posted as to where they were at all times...

Investigating the contents of the van, they found the frozen body of a young woman and eight globes containing what looked like humanoid embryos with ganglia structures attached to their heads.

The gruesome contents were confiscated and transferred to the scientific research laboratory of the FBI for further investigation.

*****

Arrest – Professors Rudolph and Melissa Maitlon
It took Bob and his team around 40 minutes to catch up with the Volvo. Eventually, they stopped the Volvo on the Artesia Freeway just after crossing Paramount Blvd.

Professor Melissa Maitlon was feisty and tried to challenge the officers. Professor Rudolph Maitlon was bewildered and just kept quiet.

The Volvo was confiscated for further investigation, and impounded when they got back to the police station.

Melissa Maitlon were placed in a cell right next to Shauna. Shauna was was not talkative at all, so the professor decided to leave her to her thoughts.

*****

The news and other main stream media was full of the story of what's happened. Stitch and Bob were everyone's heroes, and for a very long time the public talked about nothing else.

*****

Outcome for the victims

It took Judy, Grace and Burinda a while to recover after what they've been though.

Being a witness for the state, Judy had escaped a formal arrest, but she was put under constant surveillance for her own protection. The trial went on for three months, after which the perpetrators were sentenced.

Grace

Grace just took it as it came, and afterwards carried on with her life.

She'd lost the opportunity of making some money to get her and her family out of the trouble they were in, but other opportunities would come... and without the 'collateral damage' that she'd have to face, had her recent surrogating 'opportunity' turned out as it had for an unfortunate girl called 'Marna Bigado.'

A great opportunity had also arisen for Grace, helping her to improve her own financial situation, as well as that of her family, meaning that she didn't, in the end, have to follow up on any surrogacy opportunities...

Burinda

Because of the parents she was privileged to have, Burinda found it somewhat easier to recover than Judy did. And a great spin-off was the fact that she'd decided (with her father's help, of course) to begin an emotional assistance group for children who had been victims of crime, specifically crime that had involved kidnapping, abuse and neglect by their parents and drug dealing. Too many teenagers get involved in these types of crimes and it was time that somebody did something about that...

Naturally, Judy also became involved, counselling the victims. She was a natural, since she'd been a victim for such a long time...

Judy

As for Judy: she took a while to really recover. She'd suffered a lifetime of abuse by her parents and the man that hi-jacked her freedom and forced himself on her as her 'benefactor.'

Judy and Burinda became best friends. True friendship is an invaluable treasure, and for the very first time in her life, Judy had the privilege to experience true friendship. It was 'touch and go' at first, but it progressed and became better and better as time progressed.

In the end, when you put your hope in your Creator and your mind to getting up and recovering, you can do anything

In this story, the 'furnace' was extinguished for the victims who were shoved into it, and lit up for those who did the shoving.

In the end, we find Judy on the same beach that had witnessed her downfall during her youth. And in this new scenario, she really was the happy person that everybody thought she was...

Short Postlude

Midsummer, 1989.

LA, California.

Summer vacation in progress.

Scores of young people enjoying themselves on the Manhattan Beach.

In contrast, a young girl sitting alone on a beach chair, away from everybody else, reminiscing.

'If only I could turn back the clock to before all of those things happened,' she thought. 'So many bad things could've been stopped from happening... so many innocent lives could've been saved...'

The hot Californian summer sun enclosed the girl in its scorching rays, forcing her to open an umbrella.

The sound of the ocean was relaxing. She wormed her toes deep into the almost silky, but granular sand.

The girl closed her eyes and deeply breathed in the saline air of the ocean as the breakers slapped against the poles supporting the Manhattan Beach Pier.

She lazily took in the sound of the waves as they dissolved and disappeared into the sand, then came back again for more of the sand's tight cuddle.

Seagulls were frolicking in the ocean, quarrelling over morsels of food dropped by a few kids playing on the beach.

Far off, on the horizon, white, foamy clouds were assembling. Before long, they would bathe the sea and the beach in their gentle drops of rain.

"This is my most favorite place in the entire world,' thought the girl. 'I had never engaged in the opportunities that this wonderful place offers... never taken hold of the benefit of living but a

quarter of a mile from this utopia. Always 'too occupied' with other things that, in the end, never really mattered, I missed out on enjoying this beach. In future, I will make sure that I visit Manhattan Beach at least once a week... perhaps I'll find the healing here that I so desperate need... my mind and heart feel at peace here...

Epilogue

Saturday, September 17th, 1988

10 am

Marna Bigado saw the advertisement in the newspaper.

"Childless couple looking for a surrogate mom.

Couple will pay 50000 US Dollar

Please respond to Shauna Lucas – agent - on (310) 999 9999." Marna's heart skipped a beat. She'd been looking for exactly such an opportunity, since she urgently needed the money.

Marna dialed the number and waited.

"Hi, this is Shauna Lucas." Came the answer. "How may I help you?"

"Hi there," replied Marna. "My name is Marna Bigado. I saw your advertisement for a surrogate mother, and I'm interested."

"Great!" replied Shauna. "When can you come and see us?"

"How about right now?" Replied Marna. "I have some time to kill. Where are you guys?"

Marna was lucky. The research center's agent, Shauna, had agreed to pick her up at her home, not too far from the research center, and bring her through for the initial interview with Professor Melissa Maitlon...

*****

Presently, Marna was sitting in the waiting room of the research center. Two other ladies were also there.

"Marina Bigado?" said a female voice.

Marna looked up. A woman was standing in the door.

Marna stood up.

"Yes?" she said.

"I am Professor Melissa Maitlon," said the woman. "Please follow me to my office…"

She turned around and began to walk down a long passage.

Marna followed the professor, who stopped at door No 4 and opened it.

"Could you enter please?" said the professor.

Marna complied…

Inside, the professor sat down behind a desk. She beckoned Marna to sit down on the empty chair across for her.

Marna sat down, facing the professor.

"What made you apply to become a surrogate mother, Marina?" the professor wanted to know.

"I think it was simply the fact that I need the money, professor." Replied Marna. "And of course, I would be an instrument in making a childless couple happy. Oh, and please call me Marna? Everybody does…"

"Okay, Marna." Consented the professor.

"Do I need any special qualifications Professor? Marna wanted to know."

"No, Marna," replied the professor, "Except that you need to be healthy and that there be nothing wrong with your reproductive abilities."

Marna seemed relieved.

"That's great, professor," said Marna. "I am completely healthy and there is nothing wrong with my reproductive organs."

"That's good to know, Marna." Said the professor. "Of course, we will do some tests before we do any procedures."

*****

Marna's application had been successful. She was offered 50000 US Dollars to be the surrogate mother for one of the research center's client couples, Mr. and Mrs. Laurient.

The research center also offered a substantial amount as a reward, if she agreed to have the procedure done at the research center and agreed to have some tests done prior to these procedures.

The proposed reward was 1 Million US Dollars, over and above her fee of 50000 US Dollars, which was payable by the couple whose baby she was to bear...

As Marna understood it, she was about to become a surrogate mother for some childless couple's baby. The intended mother was not infertile, but a bacterial infection had created scar tissue in her fallopian tubes, causing her to be unable to conceive. Egg cells had already been extracted from her ovaries and had been fertilized using her husband's sperm.

There's nothing new about being a surrogate mother, and everything would be pretty straight forward...

Marna had jumped at the opportunity, and had agreed to all of these procedures.

*****

Presently, Marna was in the research center waiting room, waiting for he first procedure to be done. There were two other women in the waiting room with her.

'Could it be that they are here for the same program?' She wondered...'

She smiled at the women, and they smiled back, looking nervous.

'I wonder how long this is still gonna take.' She wondered...'

"Marina Bigado?" a lady called.

Marna got up.

"That's me." she said.

"Hi Marina," greeted the woman. "I'm Shauna. Please follow me."

Marna nodded, and waited for Shauna to walk so that she could follow. But Shauna took Marna's arm and began to walk. Marna had no option but to follow, but she'd accepted Shauna's act as normal procedure.

"Please call me Marna." She said.

Shauna nodded.

"Hi Marna," she said.

Marna looked back towards where she came from, and caught a glimpse of the other two women having entered the lobby and presently disappearing through the exit, giggling...

'Curious,' thought Marna. "Wonder what that was all about...'

What Marna didn't know, was that the two women had just been paid off to sit in the waiting room, looking nervous and creating the impression that they were patients waiting to be called for their procedures to be done... fact of the matter is, Marna had been recruited to complete what Grace had started; but Grace had walked out, because she grew suspicious of whatever it was that they were planning for her...

Marna and Shauna turned into a long passage. They passed an open door. Marna shivered.

'Why is the air coming from that room so cold?' Marna wondered...'

"Marna," said Shauna. "Why don't you go into room No 5 and change into the clothes provided?"

Marna nodded, and opened the door to No 5. It was empty, except for a tray on wheels that contained some instruments, an array of machines and an examination table on top of which she found a flimsy cotton pinafore and a pair of disposable paper slippers.

After removing her own clothes, she changed into the pinafore and the slippers, and then waited.

A man entered the room.

"Hi Marna, I am professor Rudolph Maitlon," he greeted and introduced himself. "You may get onto the table and lie down."

Marna complied.

"What happened to the other professor?" she wanted to know. "The lady I spoke to when I first came here?"

"That would be my wife," he explained. "Professor Melissa Maitlon. She usually does the interviewing when she doesn't do the less complicated procedures."

"I see," said Marna. "I kind of expected her to do my procedures?"

"I can see you are very nervous," said the professor.

"What procedure are you going to do on me?" Marna wanted to know.

"Just a pap smear for now, to determine if everything is indeed okay with your female parts..." replied the professor.

"But..." began Marna, but the professor interrupted her...

"Just a small procedure, Marna," he said, smiling.

'Curious,' thought Marna. 'His eyes are cold, like the eyes of a fish...'

The door opened, and the professor looked in that direction.

"Give her a small dose of Ketamine, Shauna." Said the professor. "Enough to calm her down. When we begin, we'll give her the full anesthetic."

"Right away, Professor," replied Shauna.

Shauna attached an IV to Marna's arm, and added a substance to the drip.

Marna immediately began to relax. Slowly, she felt herself drifting away

*****

Marna woke up, feeling terrible. She was in pain from her sternum right down to her hips.

"Marna," she heard her name.

She looked up, and saw Shauna standing in her bedroom door.

"Yes, Shauna?" she replied. "Is it time? I don't feel up to it, since I'm in excruciating pain."

"Yes, Marna." Said Shauna. "It's time. The pain is a normal reaction after yesterday's procedure. Please follow me. Professor Maitlon wants to discuss your embryo implantation."

"Okay," replied Marna. "No problem. Just want to put on something decent."

"Okay I'll wait," replied Shauna.

After a few minutes, Marna was ready.

"Shall we go then?" she inquired...

"Yes," said Shauna. "Let's go."

As always, Shauna took Marna's arm and began to walk

'I wonder why she always does this,' thought Marna, irritated.

They enter an office...

*****

Marna was sitting in Professor Maitlon's office, in a chair across from him, waiting to hear what he had to say.

"Well, Marna," he said. "It's almost time."

Marna smiled nervously.

"Is there anything specific that I need to know about this procedure, Professor?" She wanted to know. "I'm in excruciating pain from my sternum right down to my hips. From what I understand from the internet, it's supposed to be quite a painless, simple procedure that can be done with me being awake?"

"The pain is normal." Replied the professor. "It will dissipate after a while..."

"Okay," said Marna. "Still waiting for an answer to my question, though. Is there anything specific that I need to know about this procedure, Professor?"

"Only one thing, Marna." He replies. "I am going to implant all eight the fertilized embryos that had been fertilized by the couple involved."

"Eight!" exclaimed Marna. "Why eight?"

"We don't know if even one will attach and survive, Marna," he replied. "Implanting all eight will give you a better chance to bear a child for your clients. So, are you ready?"

For a few seconds, Marna just stared at him. Wondering whether she was misunderstanding.

"Did you say 'eight?' she wanted to confirm.

"What's wrong, Marna?" he wanted to know, his face rigid. "You look a bit overwhelmed?"

'Oh, what the heck,' she thought. 'I need this money. Let him just do it and get it over with...'

"No it's fine," she said. "Just carry on with the procedure..."

His face relaxed, and he smiled his usual smile.

"That's my girl!" he said "I knew you'd come to your senses!"

She stood up to leave his office. Strangely, she felt a bit heavy when she did that, as if she'd struggled to get up...

Marna opened the door and left the professor's office. As if on cue, Shauna was waiting for her directly outside the door. Marna looked at Shauna as she smiled.

"Okay," said Shauna. "Let's go..."

Shauna took Marna by the arm, as she always did. Previously, it didn't bother her that much. But this time, it induced fear...

"Marna," said Shauna. "Why don't you go into room No 5 and change into the clothes provided?"

Marna nodded, and opened the door to No 5. It was empty, except for a tray on wheels that contained some instruments, an array of machines and an examination table on top of which she found a flimsy cotton pinafore and a pair of disposable paper slippers.

'Dejavu,' thought Marna, but changed into the pinafore and the slippers anyway, and then waited.

The professor entered the room.

"Hi Marna," he said. "By now, you should know the drill. Get up onto the table and lie down."

Marna complied, but then began to panic.

The professor saw her mental state and recognized that it was a state of panic...

'Better do this quick,' he thought. 'Cannot afford another mess-up like with that Grace girl...!'

"Shauna," he said, "Give her a small dose of Ketamine. As yesterday, just enough to calm her down. We must to whatever we can to preserve the lives of the embryos..."

"Right away, Professor!" replied Shauna.

The IV setup had already been done, and Shauna injects the dose of Ketamine into the IV fluid that's in the bottle.

Suddenly, Marna began to panic.

'Something is not right!' she thought. 'He didn't sound very concerned about my life, he was just concerned about the embryos. I think I'd better get out of here right away!'

Somehow, she'd mustered the necessary strength and had managed to pull the IV needle from her arm. She'd jumped off of the stainless steel table and took off, running to the door…

"Oh no, not this time!" asserted the professor. He ran after her and grabbed her arm.

"Shauna, quick!" he cried. "Give her a slightly larger dose of Ketamine this time! We cannot afford to let her go. All those embryos have already attached! We need them!"

"Right away, Professor," replied Shauna. "What about the anesthetic?"

He nodded.

"When we begin, we'll give her the full anesthetic." He said. "For now, the embryos are our first priority…"

The professor dragged Marna back onto the table and held her down until the Ketamine IV hypodermic needle was attached to the vein in her arm.

Slowly, Marna began to relax…

Marna tried to focus as the Ketamine began to do its work. The room had become blurry. She saw people walking, but didn't recognize them. It sounded as though they were talking through a pipe. Everything was white, as though they were in a mist.

She could make out a scalpel coming closer toward her abdomen…

"What about the anaesthetic?" she attempted to ask, but her tongue had become thick in her mouth and she could barely open it…"

The professor looked up, then said something to Shauna… Marna could hear his voice as if through an air-filled plastic bag, but she couldn't make out the words he said.

She could hear sounds in the room, but it sounded as though the noise had to travel through thick liquid, like syrup. It sounded like drums were playing in the distance...

The professor looked Marna straight in the eye, as if he could feel her looking right at him. He said something to Shauna again, but Marna couldn't make out the words.

Two hands gripped Marna 's upper arms and pushed her back so that she couldn't look at the professor, however hard she tried...

She attempted to lift her shoulders again in order to look at the professor, but she had no strength to do that. She was compelled to compelled to stay down.

In spite of everything Marna, even in her anaesthetized condition, kept replaying the images of her surroundings, over and over, in her frightened mind... the image of the professor performing procedures on her without her consent had become especially vivid during the replays... especially the scalpel in his hand.

'Weird...' she thought, 'from the very beginning, I couldn't see him as a doctor. Now I know for sure that he's no doctor...'

Marna looked up again, seeing the scalpel getting closer, the masked face of the professor only about six inches from her face.

Unable to contain herself any longer, Marna let out a long, fearful, but soundless scream... absolutely no sound came out...

She was on the edge of an abyss and skidding... on her way to fall over the edge...

She tried her best to hold on, but she couldn't hold on anymore... she eventually let it slip and started falling into darkness...

Falling... falling... falling...

And that as the last bit of consciousness she'd ever have... her very last sensation...

*****

"I think we've lost her, Professor," said Shauna.

"Yes, we have." He replied, cold as a fish. "But we do have the foetuses, and that's what's important..."

*****

Basically, as far as Marna was concerned, this was to be a case of in vitro conception, a baby being born nine months later and a whole lot of money changing hands between the various parties.

However, two weeks later, Marna was dead.

Rest in peace, Marna...

Lightning Source UK Ltd.
Milton Keynes UK
UKHW010758051222
413416UK00016B/794